COVERT PURSUIT

A DETECTIVE SAMPSON NOVEL

DEMETRIUS JACKSON

PROLOGUE

T hunder snapped and lightning illuminated the sky as Detective Sampson pounded the pavement with each step of a dead sprint. His heart thudded against his ribcage relentlessly. Feeling taxed, he mopped rain away from his brow and silently prayed he wasn't too late.

The sounds of live music from the local watering hole assaulted his eardrums while the smells of barbecue and American pub fare tantalized his nostrils. Some partygoers ate heartily while others gyrated on each other without a care in the world. On this Friday night, North Davidson, known as NoDa to the locals, was alive and thriving.

But Detective Carl Sampson, who sprinted past the events of the evening, was singularly focused on saving the girl. He pushed his conditioning to the limit as his lungs continued to burn, but he refused to stop. An accident, caused by an SUV that slid through the intersection, forced him to get out of his vehicle and get into an all-out footrace to save the girl hidden somewhere in the city. He looked up, the commercial building in sight, and he glanced down at this watch, *seven minutes to ten.* He willed his legs to move faster, but he couldn't generate any additional power.

He'd been given clues to the girl's whereabouts and a time, 10:00 p.m., Friday night, by which he had to save her. All week he hunted down one clue after another only to come up empty handed. On this night, his final night, it was down to two locations. The abandoned paper storage facility in NoDa or the old Walmart Super Center store on Albemarle Road. After scrutinizing and evaluating each location, he settled on the paper storage facility. He wished it was some scientific process that led him to decide on this location, but it wasn't. It was his instinct and gut pulling him here.

He slowed his pace to a jog as his final strides led him to the facility's door. As he reached for the handle, the adrenaline coursing through his body caused his hand to visibly shake. He balled it into a fist to settle himself and reached out for the door again. The moisture on his palms from the constant downpour made grasping the round handle harder than necessary. Swiping his hands across his wet clothes wouldn't help, so he applied additional pressure, turned the handle, and pushed the door open.

The only light inside the building came from the moon shining through the broken glass and the periodic lightning strikes. Visibility was poor, and with the countless corners and crevasses in shadow getting a lay of the building with a quick glance was impossible. He retrieved his tactical flashlight, pressed the button, and illuminated the space in front of him.

He quietly moved with haste while clearing each room that he passed. As he moved deeper into the central core of the building, the smell of rusted pipes and stale paper swaddled him in an unyielding embrace. He strained his ears listening for a muffled yell for help or the sound of metal on concrete. As he moved, the only sounds were of him regulating his breathing.

This has got to be the right place, he thought, peering into the last room on the left. He looked down, and his watch face glowed back at him, 9:57 p.m. He picked up speed, fighting off a sinking feeling, but he was not going to give up. He would save her.

He turned the corner, prepared to walk up the stairs when his phone vibrated in his pocket. *It's too soon. I have time.* He wanted to ignore the call, but it would not change the inevitable outcome. He stopped, right foot planted on the bottom step, hand snaking into his pocket.

"Yes," he breathed into the phone.

"Detective Sampson," the voice on the other end casually said. "I hoped when I arrived this evening that my guest was gone and on her way home. But she is still here, which means you failed at your job. And unfortunately for Ms. Brianna, your failure has forfeited her life."

The muffled yells he prayed for just a few minutes prior were now echoing in his eardrums from the other end of the phone.

"You haven't done anything that can't be undone. Tell me where she is, and I'll come get her."

"That's where you are wrong. I have done things, and I can't turn—"

"I'm begging you," Sampson said, making his way in the direction of the entrance. "Let her go. Regardless of what you have done in the past, none of it matters in this moment. If you let her go, that's a life you have saved. And when someone saves a life, they are considered a hero. Why not be her hero this evening? Simply tell me where I can find her."

"No," he said flatly. "Letting her go would only exasperate the problem. It's girls like her, women like her, that think..."

He paused, carefully choosing his next words. "That think they can do whatever they want, when they want, how they want, all without any penalty. They have the world wrapped around their pinkies, and it sets a bad example. How am I to raise a child in this world when women like her exist? So you see, Detective, I gave you a fair and equitable chance to save her. I gave you the chance to be her hero. And you failed her."

"You don't have to do this!" Sampson yelled into the phone as he burst out the door into the pouring rain.

"Yes, I do," he said before terminating the connection.

1

D eep within the Driftwood Springs community, the community slept as dawn was on the horizon. However, at 735 Franklin Lane on the second floor tucked away in the nursery, Troy Evans sat rocking their daughter while singing her a song with whispered tones.

"Hush little baby, don't say a word. Daddy's going to buy you a mockingbird. And if that mockingbird wont sing, daddy's going to buy you a diamond ring."

His singing turned to humming the tune as their daughter's eyes fluttered while she prepared to drift back into her baby slumber. While he sung, he took note of how silent the room and the neighborhood was. This was his favorite time of day, because he felt this was the only time he had to himself. Even in this moment rocking in the chair and cuddling his daughter, it was still his time. His time to bond with her, reassure her that he would always be there for her and there was nothing he wouldn't do to keep her safe.

. . .

TEN MINUTES PRIOR, he was sound asleep when the whimper from the baby monitor woke him. He waited a minute to see if it was the fitful sleep that most newborns experience or if it was truly a call for help. He had his answer when the whimper turned into a cry, at which point he was a man in action. Bethany, who likely had the hardest job between the two of them, stirred with the sound.

"Don't worry, hon," he said, sliding his feet into his slippers. "I've got her. Get some rest, my love."

He padded softly from their room, down the hall, and into the nursery where the smell of baby blowout perfumed the air. If the crying hadn't woke him up, the smell surely did. He had heard from several parents to breathe through his mouth and not his nose in such situations, but he was convinced this was a joke that parents played on one another. No matter what he tried, the rotten smell assaulted his nostrils, and it didn't stop until the diaper was safely placed into the Diaper Genie.

He entered the room and walked over to his daughter's crib, where her ice blue eyes stared back at him with a frown formed on her lips.

"Good morning, Emily. What do we have here?" he asked, picking her up and moving her to the changing table. "Looks like we had a big one this evening. Oh my, much bigger than I expected."

This one, much worse than any he had seen before, bypassed the capacity of the diaper. Without a second thought, he decided this onesie wasn't worth saving and filed it away in the genie along with the diaper. After securing her in a fresh diaper and a clean onesie from the drawer, he took her to the rocker sat down and begin to rock.

. . .

NOW AS HE finished humming the melody and with his daughter fast asleep in his arms, he continued to rock and hold her as he peered out the window. The sun would be rising soon, and his neighbors would begin to stir. In fact, as he looked out of his window, he saw two women off in the distance jogging on this brisk morning. Although it was part of the lyrics, he inserted himself while singing his song, he kissed her on the forehead, and he reiterated, "I'll never let anything happen to you."

He realized he was no longer alone.

"Hey babe, is everything okay?" Bethany asked as she walked into the room.

"Yes, everything is just fine. Spending some time with my favorite girl in the world."

Enough daylight began to creep into the room for him to notice her frown of disapproval. "I thought I was your favorite girl in the world."

"No, you're my favorite woman in the world."

She inched closer and asked, "Okay, and when she becomes a woman?"

He tilted his head to the sky, "When that happens, she will be my favorite woman and you'll be my favorite old gal."

She playfully struck him in the arm before leaning in for a kiss. "Sorry I missed you get in last night. How was your weekend trip?" Before he could answer, she noticed a scratch on his chin. "And what happened here?" she asked, caressing the spot.

THROUGHOUT THE COURSE of the week, Troy informed his wife he had a conference to attend where creative writing professionals came to share ideas. He figured it would be a great way for him to network and meet more people in the area. But on that Friday night, he spent most of the evening sitting in his car, staking out the abandoned Golden Rock Brewery.

Charlotte was home to over thirty local breweries with one popping up every couple of years. As a result, the local beer scene became saturated, and thus it was survival of the fittest between the competition. Golden Rock was established three years ago and started off as the new "it" spot. It was situated in a secluded section of town, which added to its mystique. Those who visited raved about the tasty brews and the laid-back vibe. Every weekend they had live music that brought people from all around Charlotte. With well-liked beers and a thriving social scene, they were poised to take the next step. They began securing a partnership with the locally owned grocery chain, Smith's. But before they could ink the deal, tragedy befell them.

Late one Friday evening, shortly after 11:45 p.m., Marcus Neal left the establishment with his girlfriend LeAnn Wilks, his best friend Samuel Carr, and his girlfriend Eden Hill. The partygoers had an amazing time that evening drinking, dancing, and in one case taking ecstasy. Hormones raging, they decided to leave early and make their way back home. Alcohol sliding through their systems, Marcus accelerated on the curves and floored it on the straightaway. As he approached the intersection of Ward and Livingston, he decided he would drive through the light as it was turning from yellow to red. Vision blurred and depth perception compromised, he didn't roll through a yellow light, instead going through the signal that turned red four seconds prior.

At the intersection, he collided with Jerry Adams, an English teacher who was a single father of three. Marcus and Jerry were dead on impact. LeAnn, who was riding in the front seat with Marcus, flew through the window because she didn't have her seatbelt fastened. She was catapulted forty yards through the air and then slid another ten until friction brought her momentum to a stop. Samuel and Eden faired far worse; they suffered broken limbs, which kept them tethered to the car as it caught fire and burned bright until the fire department managed to get the flames under control.

Golden Rock was held liable for the death of all five lives lost that evening, since the partygoers in the car were all underage. An investigation revealed they were not checking IDs and as a result served liquor to children. They were sued by the families for wrongful death, their license was permanently revoked, and the secluded brewery closed its doors. With the stigma surrounding the building, no one wanted to touch it, and the city had not yet demolished it.

This abandoned building was where he was holding Brianna Armstrong. He really was rooting for Detective Sampson to locate the whereabouts of the girl, but he held out slim hope that it would happen. Nonetheless, he had to see it through until the end.

At 9:50 pm, he realized Sampson had failed and he walked into the building. This brewery was a location he didn't originally have on his radar. In fact, if Sampson had not visited the location while looking for the girl earlier in the week, he would not have even given it a second look. But it was indeed perfect. The detective did a thorough job of clearing the building. Checking the storage room, freezer, and each of the brewery tanks. With the effort he put into crossing this location off the list, having it as the scene of the crime was in a manner, poetic.

In his haste to position the girl for her rescue or her more likely demise, he hadn't secured the restraint on her right wrist enough. When he disconnected the call with Sampson and she was facing certain death, she pulled against her bindings with an inhuman surge of strength and freed her hand.

Upon noticing this, Troy rushed to the table to prevent her from freeing herself completely. Like an animal that was cornered, she valiantly fought, keeping her attacker at bay. But with only one hand free, she could either attack or free herself. Each time she reached for her binding, Troy inched closer, and she went back to manically scratching at the air. The look of desperation burned from her eyes as she continued to look for a way to free herself. When she reached for her binding a fourth time, Troy lunged at her. He was quick, but in this instance she was quicker. She managed to scratch him along the chin before he was able to regain control of her wrist. "You're going to wish you hadn't done that," he said, fixing the restraint. As he did, a single tear rushed down her cheek, and all the fight she had left in her dissipated.

"THE TRIP WAS GOOD," he said answering Beth. "The networking didn't go exactly as expected—the guest of honor didn't arrive in time—but the remainder of us were able to connect and engage in an intellectual debate about the current state of academia. As for the scratch, I cut myself shaving the night of the opening ceremonies."

"Well, that looks fairly deep. You really need to be careful when you shave. Those blades can be really sharp."

"As always, you are right, and honestly I'd probably lose my head if it wasn't attached to my shoulders. Anyway, you should go get another hour or so of rest before she is up and ready to start her day. I wouldn't mind spending a few more minutes with her before I need to prepare for work."

Bethany smiled, kissed him on the cheek once again, and said, "You don't have to tell me twice." She returned to the bedroom.

Prior to picking up the hum once again, he listened to the rhythmic breathing of Emily Ann and thought, Yes, *I do need to be more careful. I cannot afford any slip-ups going forward.*

2

D etective Carl Sampson removed his sunshades upon entering the Charlotte Metro Police Department HQ. Front desk Sergeant John Bellows was the first to encounter Sampson as he entered the building. The bloodshot eyes and gloomy mood didn't escape the Sergeant, who nonetheless said, "Good morning, Carl."

Sampson acknowledged the greeting with a head nod and a grunt as he slugged his to his desk. As he entered the detective's floor, the smell of last night's over-heated coffee permeated throughout the floor, and the ambient conversation from his fellow detectives filled the air. His goal for the day was to stay out of the way and focus his energy's on finding the bastard who had surely killed Brianna. When he thought about it, he realized he didn't even know her last name, but he feared she was already out of his reach.

He pulled his phone from his pocket, opened the gallery app, and eyed the grainy picture of the girl he failed to save. He dropped his full weight into his office chair, dropped the phone on his desk, and propped his head into his hands. He tried to clear his mind, but the words from the killer rung in his ears. "I gave you the chance to be her hero. And you failed her." The tighter he pushed his head into his palms, the louder the words echoed.

He slowly leaned back in his chair as a decision was setting firmly in his mind. He could sit here and be the failure that his mind taunted, or he could dedicate every breath he took to finding this sick, sadistic son of a bitch. He decided on the latter and pondered the best place to start.

There were already subtle differences between the case of Mandy Cox and what he knew about the missing, now presumed dead, Brianna. While he knew the body of Mandy had been moved, the belief all along was her death took place somewhere in Asheville. From everything he knew about the current victim, she was being held somewhere local. He had also been given a proof of life prior to the ultimatum of the deadline to save her. But the biggest change of all was the killer's willingness to engage him in conversation.

These stark differences put a thought in the back of his mind that it was a different killer, but his gut told him this was the same person. But what he couldn't reconcile was the change in MO. *He's an amateur,* Sampson thought and wrote it at the top of his notes. He was likely still finding his way and thus would be more unpredictable. With his thumb on his temple, Sampson tapped his forehead trying to squeeze out additional thoughts.

While there were some differences, he had to acknowledge the similarities. Both women were about the same age, same body type, and... he tapped harder, trying to think. It was right on the edge of his consciousness and refused to surface when he heard commotion coming from the floor.

He looked up to see the desk to see the sergeant escorting someone through a sea of onlookers. When they turned to come in his direction, he caught a glimpse of who it was.

Detective Elise Porter, the detective he worked with to apprehend Hugo Wolfe. *What is she doing here? Did the body of
Brianna show up in Asheville? Could I have been wrong about the
premises I just laid out?*

She was different than he recalled. She walked tall on two-
inch heels and a discernible air of confidence. Her black
trousers and a red and black striped blouse were tailored to fit
her figure. Speckled red and black glasses framed her face,
and her straight blonde hair swung carefree just above her
shoulders.

She smiled upon seeing him, and he did the same. He
prepared to greet her when the sergeant kept her moving past
him and his prepared "hello." It was then he turned around
and saw his boss, Captain Marshall, brimming with a smile on
his face as well. *Was the smile for me or for him?* It didn't matter.
What mattered was the purpose for her visit. He had a ton of
questions racing through his mind, but answers wouldn't be
forthcoming until she finished with the captain.

He watched as Porter and Marshall shook hands and
disappeared into his office. Sampson prepared to slump back
into his seat when he heard, "Sampson, with me." His
momentum carried him to the seat, but he bounced back to
his feet.

It was no secret he and Captain Marshall didn't see eye to
eye. They regularly butted heads on the direction Sampson
took to solve his cases. On numerous occasions, he found
Marshall would butt in where his opinion or directives were
unwarranted. But that never stopped him. He stepped in the
middle and made claims to the press that Sampson found
himself at odds with more times than not.

"Coming, Captain," he said as he followed in their wake.
His mind shifted gears. He was sure the body was found in
Asheville, and since he and Porter worked the case previously,

her superiors likely wanted to have the two detectives work the case once again. He shuttered when he thought about the scene they would walk into or the pictures that had already been taken.

Since Sampson was the last person into the office, Marshall said to him, "Close the door behind you and take a seat." Marshall turned his attention to Porter. "Can I offer you anything to drink?" he asked.

"No, sir," she answered, sliding into the chair from him and crossing her legs.

Sampson sat in the chair next to Porter, wary of the reason for the meeting.

"Detective Porter, I hope your trip back to Charlotte was a quick and painless one."

"Yes, sir, it was. I arrived last night, settled into my hotel room, and I'm prepared for today. Traffic was minimal and the drive was easy."

"Well, don't get to use to it. The traffic within the city can turn into gridlock for no apparent reason."

She smiled and said, "I'm sure I can handle it, but consider me forewarned."

"Now," Marshall said, clearing his throat, "let's get down to business. I received the papers from your former captain on Friday, so the transfer is official. I'm happy to have someone with your experience and drive joining our department."

Joining our department. Does that mean...

"Your work to help us put away Hugo Wolfe for the mutilation and death of Mandy Cox was top notch, something Sampson could learn from."

The two locked eyes, and just like that Sampson could feel his blood beginning to simmer.

"In an effort to make the best use of our current roster, I've decided I'm going to partner you with Detective Sampson here. He can show you around the city, and you can show him how to be a top-rate detective."

The simmering feeling was quickly rising to a boil, but he refused to take the bait. He looked over at Porter and thought he saw a hint of discomfort.

"Well, sir, I'm honored to be a part of the team, and I look forward to working with Detective Sampson. When we teamed up for our last case, I learned more from him than I think he learned from me. I think our partnership can grow, and I just know we will be a kick-ass team."

Marshall looked over at Sampson, "Is there anything you would like to add, Detective?"

His head was still spinning from the news. Coming into the office today, this was not what he expected. "Welcome to the team," he said.

A knock at the door broke the awkward silence that was filling the room.

"Yeah, who is it?" Marshall asked with a tinge of irritation.

The door swung open and Officer Johnson poked his head through the door. "Captain, this just came over the wire. The body of a young girl was found in the old Golden Rock Brewery."

Sampson instantly felt his stomach sour at its mention. His mind raced, *this can't be her. I checked this location, and it was completely empty.*

Johnson continued, "From what we've been able to gather, it's a college aged girl..."

No, don't say it, Sampson thought.

"Sir, her skin has been removed and she was left sitting in the middle of the ground floor."

Sampson knew the shoe would fall, but he didn't expect it to be at a location he searched prior to the expiration of the time limit.

"A tip came into the hotline that the body of a girl had been found. First officers on the scene thought it unlikely, but from the reports over the radio, it's a pretty gruesome sight."

The seated occupants looked at each other. Marshall was the first to speak, "Are you sure about this, Johnson?"

"Yes, sir, I personally called the officer on the scene, and he confirmed the transmission."

"Does this mean we have a copycat out on the streets?" Marshall asked rhetorically. "Sampson, Porter, this is your case. Find out why we are seeing the same MO in the death of this unidentified girl that mimics that of the person you put behind bars."

"You've got it, sir," Porter said.

"We're on it, Captain," Sampson said.

They stood and walked out of the captain's office. Porter was the first to speak, "Do you think? Is it possible we have a copycat on our hands?"

Sampson thought about confiding in his new partner that the killer was still walking the streets. He broached his reservations when they locked Hugo away previously, but she refused to believe it could have been anyone else. Confiding in her with what he knew would do no good without proof. So no, he wouldn't confide in her. Not until he had something tangible that proved the person locked away was not responsible for the death of Mandy and the person who committed this murder was not a copycat.

"Anything is possible," he said. "I think it's best we let the clues lead us to a decision and for us not to formulate one until we have all the facts."

Porter eyed her new partner. "You're right." With a smile, she asked, "Who's driving?"

On this warm sunny day, the campus at the University of North Carolina Charlotte, UNCC, was once again abuzz after the weekend break. Students meandered from dormitories to class, hustled from class to class, or simply sat around soaking up the rays. Professors taught the eager minds and future leaders of tomorrow, elated when the lightbulb went off after discussing complex topics like quantum theories or advanced algorithms.

The campus wildlife wasted no time getting into the act. The birds' melodies serenaded each other from one side of campus to the other. And squirrels played tag as they raced about simultaneously avoiding contact with human passersby.

The smell of fresh-cut grass permeated the air from the ground's crew early morning efforts. Inside of Crown Commons dining hall, pineapple curry chicken was being gobbled up and being washed down with sweet tea by those sitting down for a meal.

All said, there couldn't be a more perfect way to start the academic week. And on the second floor inside of Carnegie Hall, Professor Troy Evans agreed for vastly different reasons.

The death of Brianna meant another book in which his main character, Dillon, outwitted the police while ridding the world of another unscrupulous harlot. It was Dillon who gave him the idea and strength to place the body in a location where Sampson had already paid a visit. Troy thought this tactic risky, but Dillon didn't see risk, merely another challenge to overcome. Troy had to admit, the idea was brilliant, and the fans of Dillon would savor this devious twist.

Speaking of fans, it was the beginning of the week, which meant time to review both sales and reviews from the previous week. In the first two weeks of his debut novel, The Binds that Tie under the pseudonym William Stealth, he barely saw any traction. Each hour of the day he found himself checking to see if there were any new sales. For each sale, he anxiously waited to see if the reader would leave a review. He often wondered how long it took to read a book. One week, two weeks? He knew it depended on the speed of the reader. Nonetheless he thought he could calculate it given enough time.

He logged into his author account, still devoid of a picture, and navigated to the recent sales page. His default setting, the previous seven days, allowed him to review his sales from the week. The page took longer than normal to load, so he looked over at his sales from two weeks ago, eight ebooks and two paperbacks. *Decent for an unknown author*, he thought as the screen began to redraw with the updated data. He scanned it, anxious to see the improvement over the last set. Twelve ebooks and zero paperbacks, a net two improvement. *A small victory, but a victory nonetheless*. He navigated to the Reviews tab and again waited on the drastically slow connection to pull the data and populate the screen.

The silence he'd been enjoying was interrupted with scraping coming from next door. It took him a moment, and then he realized they were removing his former colleague's name. Hugo Wolfe had been a womanizing adulterer who fornicated with Mandy Cox in exchange for increasing her grades. She'd flaunted herself to get ahead instead of applying herself. He'd succumbed to her advances and violated the code of conduct with regards to teacher and student relationships. Oh, the audacity they had to act on their carnal urges in the office that was less than ten feet from his own. Their torrid relationship and lack of decency made him sick to his stomach.

As Charlie the maintenance man worked to remove Hugo's name from the door, Troy was proud for removing him from the university and out of the reach of other students. And even more proud of ridding the world of someone like Ms. Cox.

He refocused his energies on the screen and the reviews for his book. He maintained the default sort order, newest to oldest, and observed there were a few new reviews. The first review was from Lewis Redd from South Dakota.

"OMG! One of the best books I've read in the last two years. I could totally feel the hairs on the back of my neck raise as Dillon meticulously stalked his prey. The women taking advantage of their wealthy husbands' long working hours got exactly what they deserved in the end. I can't wait to read what Dillon has in store for them in his next book."

A smile crept over Troy's features as he reread the review. It was always refreshing for a reader to understand where the author was going and that they appreciated the hard work he poured into the novel. He had no doubt Lewis would love the next entry in the Dillon Series.

He moved onto the next review from Lisa Standsberry from South Carolina.

"One star! If I could give it zero I would, but since I don't have the option, one it is. Author William Stealth does a terrible job building his characters and their world. The main character Dillon is a complete tool, killing women because he sees them cheating on their well-to-do husbands. If it bothered him that much, he could have simply called the husband and let him know. For all the four-and-five-star reviews on this book, it makes me wonder how twisted people in this world have become. I certainly will not be reading another one of his books."

Troy's initial response would have been to fly off the handle at such a rebuke of his work. But Dillon equipped him with better means to deal with rejection. For such a harsh review, he pondered if the book hit too close to home for Mrs. Standsberry. Maybe she was having an affair that she didn't want her husband to know about. Maybe she wondered about her own safety.

"Well, Ms. Standsberry, maybe one day you and I will cross paths. At which time you can see for yourself how this world is truly built."

The voice in his head urged him caution and patience. It urged him to ignore the personal attacks and instead see this as an opportunity for growth. He knew the voice was right. It was always right. *Consider yourself lucky, Lisa,* was his final thought on the matter.

To keep himself from getting into more of a fit than he found himself at the moment, he moved away from the reviews and to the main reason he logged into his author account for the morning.

The second book in the Dillon Series was ready to be uploaded for public consumption. He took his time entering the required metadata.

Author Name: William Stealth

Book Title: The Binds that Restrain

Series Name: Dillon

Volume: 2

Book Description: From the author of The Binds that Tie comes the second novel in the Dillon Series. After pointing the detectives in the wrong direction and pinning the murder on the victim's lover, Dillon is back to right more wrongs. The Binds that Restrain will navigate you through the twist and turns as our main character is doing everything possible to stay one step ahead of the police. Can he allude capture once again and leave another victim for the police to find, or will the woman be saved and him incarcerated for her kidnapping?

Categories: Psychological Thriller, Domestic Thriller, Thriller Suspense, Crime

He then moved onto uploading the final manuscript and setting the price for his latest masterpiece. The process from submission to release took on average three days, so by Thursday his growing fanbase would have their hands on his latest work, and he could officially begin plotting his next novel.

In books one and two, Dillon's targets were the women who came into the auto repair shop. But there were more women out there doing wrong other than those who walked through his door. Dillon, an apex predator, needed to hunt bigger game. He needed to widen his pool. He needed prey who would be a challenge to apprehend, to subdue, to be worthy of time, energy, and efforts. One thing for sure, the prey had to be a professional, working woman.

Several thoughts swam through his mind. Abduct the dean of the local college whose husband ran a global consulting firm and spent most of his time traveling. Meanwhile she's having a secret love affair with her handsome pool boy. It was a viable option, but he didn't want to latch onto his first thought.

He then considered abducting a local TV personality just before she goes on air. Her husband runs a tech company, yet she finds time to stay after hours to get it on with her camera man in studio six.

He believed in having at minimum three options to choose from, and at present he only has those two. Therefore, he needed another one before he would make his decision. He could feel an idea percolating at the edge of his consciousness, but it had not pushed its way to the forefront just yet. He would be patient and would allow the thought to form on its own, because something in the back of his mind told him this would be the best option of them all.

4
———

Detectives Carl Sampson and Elise Porter arrived at the crime scene shortly after 9:00 a.m. Porter was on the phone throughout the course of the drive. The first two calls came from her former colleagues wishing her well on her first day.

Melissa Ringer, who graduated the academy with Porter, was the second of the two calls and monopolized the conversation. She walked down memory lane from their days into the academy and everything they went through to be the newest set of first-grade detectives within their department. With Porter's departure, she was now the sole woman, since Gillian retired last fall.

Porter assured her everything would be perfectly fine, and in fact there were two female officers who took the detective's exam. She reviewed their stellar resumes prior to exiting, and there was a strong likelihood they would both be promoted to detective provided they excelled on the exam. Ringer wanted to continue, but another caller interrupted their conversation.

This call was from a local realtor who had been searching for a property that Porter could call home. Although Sampson could only hear one side of the conversation, it was clear she found three properties she wanted to show his new partner. Porter advised her a hot case had just fallen into her lap that she needed to address immediately. He sensed frustration from the realtor as Porter's next response seemed to be more on the defensive side. In the end, they compromised on viewing the properties tomorrow evening.

By the time the conversation concluded, Sampson had bypassed the news crews already on the scene and searched for a spot to park his department-issued Ford Explorer. He had to admit it was a welcome step up from old Betsy. He shifted the vehicle into park and looked over to his new partner.

"You ready?" he asked as she stowed her phone.

"As ready as I'll ever be," she responded. While she wasn't a new detective, this was her first case as a detective in this department. In the previous case she worked with Sampson, she was playing with house money with regards to Captain Marshall. Now she needed to perform for a captain she had not worked for. Every boss had their idiosyncrasies, and it took time to learn them. But one thing was common amongst each of them, they expected results. Therefore, if she did her job and closed the cases, then that was one less thing she needed to worry about.

"Let's go," Sampson said, pulling on the handle and opening the door. A gust of stifling hot air pushed its way into the climate-controlled interior of the Explorer. Sampson exited the vehicle, Porter did the same, and they grouped at the front by the hood.

Instantly the questions from the reporters were fired in their direction.

"Detectives, who is the victim and why were they left here?"

"How long has the victim been in this abandoned location?"

"Is this a cold case you can now close and provide closure to a grieving family?"

Sampson allowed each question to bounce off him and responded with, "No comment," as they continued to move away from the story seekers.

Jointly they strode in the direction of the brewery, where the crime scene tape had been stretched across the door roughly four and a half feet high. The officer standing post outside watched as they approached.

"Detectives Sampson and Porter," he said, both showing their credentials to the officer.

"They're expecting you inside," he said, lifting the tape and allowing them passage. Sampson still needed to duck under it, but it was lifted just high enough to allow Porter to walk beneath it without the need to duck.

It didn't take long to ascertain the answer to the second question. The ripe smell of new death was fresh in the air. Sampson figured the heat of the last few days cooked the body even more, thus adding to the rancid aroma. A fellow detective told him once that you eventually get used to the smell, but the pungent odor of death was something he knew he would never get used to for as long as he lived.

The crime scene technicians had numbered tents strategically placed around the body and lined them up in focus to snap pictures of anomalies or things they found of interest. As Sampson and Porter grew closer, the realization gripped him when he saw the mutilated body. There was no doubt in his mind it belonged to that of Brianna, and that final hope that she was still alive evaporated.

Brandy Brown, the county's medical examiner, approached the arriving detectives. "Good morning, Sampson," she said with familiarity. "Who do you have with you today?"

"Hey Brandy, this is my new partner, Detective Elise Porter. She transferred in from Asheville, and today is her first day."

"Hell of a way to start day one," Brandy said, reaching out to shake Porter's hand. "Nonetheless, welcome."

"Thank you," Porter said, shaking her hand. "What have you determined thus far?"

"Well, our victim is a female roughly 18-22 years old. Her skin has been removed from her body with surgical precision. Her hair has been cut from her head and left in the bag situated next to her. We haven't opened the bag, but we could see strands purposefully left protruding through the closed zipper."

Both Sampson and Porter looked in the direction of the body and noticed the bag for the first time. Sampson asked, "Do you know how long she has been dead?"

Brandy hesitated slightly before saying, "The increased heat may have caused the body to decompose at a faster rate than natural, but if I had to venture a guess, I'd say two days, maybe three."

Sampson was not surprised by this answer. In fact, he knew the final findings would show she was killed between 10:00 p.m. Friday night and 2:00 a.m. Saturday morning. It just depended on how long it took the bastard to do all of this. He silently gave her, Brianna, a prayer for peace, since he hadn't been fast enough to save her from this horrible fate.

"I'll be able to provide a firm timeframe once I get her back and perform the autopsy. Give me a couple of days and I will have an answer for you."

"Thanks, Brandy," he said as they parted ways. Both detectives moved in unison toward the body. Seeing her on display like this brought Sampson's hatred to a new level. He didn't believe in vigilante justice. He believed in the system along with the checks and balances that were put into place. But in this moment, as he looked at the mutilated corpse of Brianna, he could see himself placing a bullet right between the eyes of this coward.

Porter, who had been quiet for most of the exchange, said, "Looks like our copycat did his homework. The only discernible difference I see at the moment is the location of the body dump."

Sampson wanted to scream. *It's not a copycat, it's the same damn perp. And he selected this venue to taunt me. But how*, he thought. *How did he know I had already been here? Could he be watching me? Could he have been playing me this entire time? Did he ever plan on me finding her in any state other than the one he has put on display today?*

"Sampson," he heard as Porter had repositioned herself to stand in front of him. "Are you okay?"

"Yeah, I'm fine. Let's check the bag to see if there are any other clues." He led them over to the bag and slipped on a pair of gloves before taking a knee next to it. The bag was black and grey with straps that allowed a front closure in addition to the straps that allowed the users to carry it on their back. It had three zipper compartments and two mesh pockets on either side, presumably to hold drinks.

Sampson unzipped the first compartment. Inside he found a black leather wallet closed with a snap. He unlatched it, and smiling back at him was the picture of Brianna Armstrong front and center on her driver's license. *Armstrong. Your last name is Armstrong.* He handed the wallet over to his partner and rummaged through the remainder of that compartment. Other than pockets for pens and other knick-knacks, it was empty.

He moved onto the second compartment, the one in which

the blonde hair had been caught in the zipper. He cautiously unzipped the compartment to find it filled with the victim's hair. He wasn't sure what it all meant other than they were dealing with a sick individual.

He moved to the last compartment, already prepared for what he assumed was inside. He hesitated at the zipper, willing himself to open it. When he did, the skin that had been removed from Brianna Armstrong's body had been placed in the largest and final compartment. He zipped it back up and stood. Porter did the same.

As they did, Porter spoke, "Brianna Armstrong, 18 years old from Raleigh, North Carolina. Long way from home."

"Indeed, it is, but not far enough apparently. There's not much more for us to uncover here, but we do need to go and notify the family."

Porter eyed him wearily, "Can't the local police handle the notification?"

"They could, but we will need to take a trip up there at some point. We can kill two birds with one stone."

She acquiesced, and they walked in the direction of the exit. Prior to exiting the brewery, Sampson called out to the ME, "I'd like the report as soon as it's ready."

"You've got it, Carl. Good to meet you, Detective," she said to their departing forms.

Back outside, they were once again accosted by the media.

"Detective Sampson, you've got to tell us something. Was the victim male or female? Do you have a name?"

Porter was the one to stop and she said, "A young girl has been found dead. That is all we are at liberty to say."

"Do you have a name?" another reporter asked.

"We will need to notify next of kin. Until then no additional information will be shared."

Another series of questions were lobbed their way as they

slid into the Explorer. Sampson started the vehicle, where the cool air from the vents blasted them in the face. He placed the car into gear, performed a U-turn, and headed back to the main road.

This was the first moment they had alone in which they were not bothered by interruptions. He pointed the nose of the car in the direction of the freeway and asked, "What made you take this position?"

"Nothing made me take the position," she corrected him. "I asked for a transfer. I love Asheville. It's a great city with rich history and amazing eateries. But the police department is small in comparison to that of the CMPD. The truth is the opportunity for advancement didn't look promising. I either needed the right connections and backing to be in the running or someone higher up had to vacate the position. When I looked at the landscape, I didn't see anyone retiring soon and didn't feel like dealing with those politics."

He thought back to the numerous conversations he had with Captain Marshall. It was always clear to him the captain was working an angle. One in which he could leverage to jettison his current position in exchange for a new one when the time came.

"I'd recommend caution. The politics around here can be cutthroat."

She appeared to ponder it for a while and said, "It's true you'll run into politics wherever you go, but the pond is much bigger here."

"And bigger ponds come with more relentless sharks."

The comment seemed to hang in the air with nowhere to go. Sampson diverted the conversation, "How do you want to handle the notification?"

Porter smiled, "Well, since you handle the last one so well, why don't you take this one too?"

He grunted and said, "Of course," as he settled in behind the wheel for the drive out to Raleigh.

5

"Hon, I have been waiting for this all day long," Bethany gushed while Troy parked the car. "Luigi's is my favorite pizza joint of all time. The home-made dough. The fresh mozzarella. The hand-cut large pepperonis that sizzle and curl at the edges from the heat of the oven. And don't even get me started on the cheesy garlic bread with flecks of chopped garlic. Look at me," she implored, pointing to herself. "I'm drooling just thinking about how much I am going to eat when we walk in."

Troy shifted the lever into park and said, "Had I known I would have gotten this type of reception, I would have recommended this outing earlier."

"Troy, it came right on time. Being a parent has been life altering and amazing, but I crave some adult time and conversation. By the way, are we getting a supreme or our traditional pepp and onion? Or maybe something new. Oh, I've got it. Let's get a pie for here and then one to take home. I bet it tastes just as good reheated in the oven as when we'll have it tonight."

Troy let out a hearty laugh as he walked around the car to

open the passenger side door. "Alright now. Let's not get ahead of ourselves. Why don't we start with the one pie and if you're still gung-ho about a second one, then we'll order it to go."

"You can wait all you want, but that second pie will be making its way home with us."

The couple walked in the direction of the restaurant with Beth leaning into her husband while they held hands. Upon entering, Troy said, "Table for two please."

"Right this way," the hostess said, leading them to a booth in the corner. She placed the menus on the table and before turning to leave said, "Your server will be over in just a moment to take your drinks. Enjoy."

"Drinks," Bethany exclaimed. "I should have a drink too."

"Only if you want our helpless daughter drunk off mommy's milk."

She seemed to ponder the statement and although the risk was minimal she said, "Well, I want a milkshake."

"I'll see what I can do, but no promises."

Each of the three TVs in Luigi's were turned to sports. A college basketball game was midway through the first half. The second was tuned to the NBA contest preparing to tip-off between the Denver Nuggets and the Charlotte Hornets. The last one was on Sports Center, which was showing highlights from the Nascar race from the previous day.

The restaurant had a semi-open concept that allowed them to see some but not all of the work going on in the kitchen. The view delighted all the children, who saw the dough flung into the air, rotating roughly 1080 degrees before being caught on a fist and sent skyward again. The other visible attraction was the various devices used to slice and dice the fresh produce and meats.

Patrons enjoyed Luigi's for more than the great pizza. They came in and sat down to relish the light, fun, family experience. But on this Monday evening, the teaser for the late-night news broke the mood and grabbed the attention of many in the establishment that night.

"Breaking News at 11:00. Today officers found the body of a young girl in the old Golden Rock Brewery. Detectives working the case are being tight lipped about the details, but sources within the department say the scene was more gruesome than anything they've seen before. Tune in at 11:00 for the latest."

Bethany had been prepared to take another bite from her slice when she suddenly stopped and dropped it back on her plate. "What on Earth is this world coming to? Young girls being murdered by these, these savages. It's bad enough we have psychos shooting up our schools and now we have people gruesomely murdering young girls. How the hell will we keep our daughter safe from these predators? I tell you, I hope they find the son of a bitch and do to him whatever was done to that poor girl."

In a semi-detached voice, Troy said, "Our system of justice doesn't believe in an eye for an eye."

"Well, they should! Then these creeps would probably think twice about committing such heinous crimes. And the family that is left to deal with the loss of their loved one. How do they find the strength to go on?"

"I would imagine it's probably really tough for them," he said while simultaneously thinking, *their families may care, but the world is still better off without them.* "The truth is there are so many levels of evil in the world. Some are right there for people to see, while others are overt and hidden within plain sight. I submit one is not any worse than the other."

"They are all wrong. Overt or blatantly obvious. The world should not have to deal with these sickos."

Involuntarily Troy's eye twitched at the rebuke and harsh

words levied by his wife. *Tread lightly*, the voice in his head said. *Change topics,* it urged. "You're right, hon, and it looks like you're slowing down. Is it time to order that second pie?"

"No, I don't have the appetite anymore. Let's just pay the bill and head home. I suddenly feel the need to hold my baby girl in my arms and protect her from the crazies outside our home."

Troy signaled for the waiter, "Can we get the check when you get a chance?"

The waiter opened the leather case that was tucked away in his apron pocket, found the tab belonging to the couple, and sat it face down on the table between the two of them.

Troy swiped it up, reviewed the different line items for accuracy, and then pulled thirty dollars from his wallet. "Come on, sweetheart. Let's head home." He stood, walked over to her, and pulled the chair back slightly so she could stand. As he did, the door opened, and walking into the restaurant was Detective Sampson and from the looks of it another detective. He watched as Sampson mouthed, "just two this evening." The same woman who sat him and Bethany led the detectives in their direction.

Bethany stood and obscured the view as the trio walked by. He guided her by the small of her back to the exit. He noticed a spike of adrenaline as they did. He didn't know if it was from seeing the detective in person again or if it was from the sight of his new partner.

"I STILL DESPISE DEATH NOTIFICATIONS," Sampson said, parking the Explorer in the parking lot for Luigi's. "There's always that awkward moment after the notification when I'm not sure what to do next. Do you hug the grieving family member or give them the space to cry it out? Nothing feels right, and it all seems unnatural. Sure, the manual advises to keep your distance, but it's in those moments I think they need the human connection for the loss they just experienced."

"I typically try to find something else to bring them comfort. For some, simply asking them to let you help them make coffee or tea helps. This is something they do on automatic if they've done it for years. It allows them to feel they are being productive and not focused on their grief."

They opened the vehicle doors and stepped out, "That's not a bad idea. I'll have to try that some time."

"Now," she said changing the subject. "What's the deal with this place?"

"Hands down the best pizza in town. Everything sourced fresh and never frozen. You'll swear you died and went to heaven."

Porter laughed as they walked in. It was a good sign that the place was three-fourths full, and looking back into the kitchen there was a good number of pies waiting to be picked up by hungry families.

"Can I help you?" the hostess asked.

"Just two this evening," Sampson said

"Right this way." She led the detectives to the back of the restaurant. "Will this booth be okay?"

"It's perfect. Thank you," Sampson responded.

"Your waiter will be with you shortly. Enjoy," she said as she made her way back to her post.

They both slid in across from one another. Porter picked up the menu, reviewing the options. "So, what do you suggest detective?"

"What wouldn't I suggest is the better question. Everything I've had has been top notch. But since you are new in town, you get to choose."

"I'm thinking anchovies and mushrooms," she said, peering over the top of her menu.

"Well in that case..."

"Just kidding. I'm good with pepperoni and sausage."

"Haha. Everybody's a comedian."

The waiter appeared to take their drink orders, and since they were ready he accepted their pizza order as well.

Sampson picked the conversation back up, "The Armstrong's mentioned that the day Brianna went missing she attended a birthday party for her best friend. At the time she wasn't dating anyone."

"Yeah, but that doesn't necessarily rule out a boyfriend. I've been a teenage girl, and there are certain truths we don't tell our parents. I suggest we pull her phone records to see who she'd been talking to prior to her disappearance."

"Agreed, because that is something that has been troubling me. How did she end up in Charlotte? Her car was in the garage, so unless someone came to pick her up, she would not have had the means to travel down here."

"Unless she got an Uber to the train station and took the Amtrak. Dumb love can get you to do dumb things."

Sampson took a drink of his Coke. "But her parents said she has always been levelheaded. So, while it's possible, it's hard to believe she would have made such a poor decision."

"I don't see how her and the killer could have crossed paths. Maybe our copycat wanted to find someone out of the area and bumped into her somehow."

Sampson scrunched his face up in concentration. "She was a senior, right?"

"Yep. Why do you ask?"

"Part of being a senior is preparing to move on to the next stage in your life. For some it's finding a trade or finding them-selves. But for most it's preparing for college. Mandy was a student at UNCC when she went missing. What if our killer met her on a college campus?"

"That makes sense, but she wasn't in college yet."

"Yeah, nonetheless let's see if we can get a list of all the colleges she applied to. It's a lead worth chasing at least."

The waiter came back with a pizza stand and two plates. "Your order will be just a few more minutes. Can I refill your drink?" he asked motioning to Sampson's half empty glass.

"Yes, thank you."

"Can you look into securing the phone records?" he asked Porter.

"First thing tomorrow morning."

"Good, I'll take the college angle. I'm sure we'll turn up something." He pulled his glass from the table and tapped it twice on the tabletop. "Enough about the case for tonight. Since we're officially partners and all, why don't you tell me more about yourself."

"Ehh," she said with an exasperated sigh. "I really don't like to talk about myself."

"Come on. We are going to be spending a lot of time together. We need something to talk about other than our cases."

She evaded the question by saying, "There really isn't much to tell."

"Something is better than nothing," he persisted.

"Fine. I'm the oldest of three children. My dad passed away my second year in college. My mom works as a psychiatrist, and she has her own practice. I live alone and don't like cats. There, that's me in a nutshell."

"How riveting. I'll let you off the hook tonight, but I want to hear more. From the conversation you had on the phone, sounds like you are looking for a place to live."

"Yes, and it's turning out to be harder than I imagined.

Right now, I'm staying in a hotel, but of course that can't last forever. I'm working with a realtor who came highly recommended. She's found three properties she wants to show me."

"You should go see them. If you don't, they are bound to be gone before you know it."

"We are scheduled to go tomorrow after work. Speaking of going to see something. I just had a thought. What would it take to go see Hugo? Maybe he can shed some light on who the copycat is."

Sampson groaned inwardly, because he knew damn well Mr. Wolfe wouldn't have any information that could move the case forward. Especially if they went in asking about a copycat killer. "I imagine we could send a request to the warden, and he could grant us permission. We may need to run it past his attorney as well."

"I think it would be worthwhile to pay him a visit. I'll call up there tomorrow while I'm obtaining the phone records."

Great, he thought knowing the visit to see Hugo would be forthcoming. The appearance of the pizza allowed him to keep his thoughts to himself. Instead, he pulled a slice of pizza from the tray and placed it on Porter's plate. He then grabbed a slice for himself and said, "Bon appetit."

6

You know what you need to do. Don't waste this opportunity, the voice inside of Troy's head said. Beth hadn't said much since they left Luigi's, and that didn't matter to Troy. He was concentrating on the decision he needed to make by the time they reached their home. He made the final turn onto their street and pulled into the driveway. While he waited on the garage door to open, he decided the time was now.

"Damn it. I left my wallet at the restaurant. I'll head back now."

"Sure," Beth said as she stepped from the vehicle into the garage.

He backed from the driveway, shifted the car into park, and the hunt was on. Luigi's wasn't far from the Evans' home, therefore Detective Sampson and his partner would still be enjoying their pizza by the time he arrived. His wallet, tucked away in his back pocket, was the convenient excuse to execute his plan for the evening.

Troy, the consummate meticulous planner, felt he was flying by the seat of his pants. But he acknowledged he wouldn't obtain a more perfect opportunity. Jumbled thoughts raced through his mind and it required focus on his part to slow them into coherent ones. For the plan he was formulating he couldn't rush it; he had to take his time. But tonight would be phase one. Phase one of a multifaceted plan.

He arrived at the parking lot as the two detectives were exiting the building. He headed toward the back of the lot. One to stay out of the sightline of his prey and also to reposition the vehicle to point in the direction of the exit. He watched as the female detective slurped the last of her milkshake, the milkshake that was meant for Beth. She tossed the empty cup into the trash bin located outside the entrance. He watched as they disappeared into the police-issued Explorer. The brake lights shone briefly as Sampson started the car and put it into drive. Troy could feel the condensation on his palms as he gripped the steering wheel and pressed the accelerator.

The high profile of the SUV made it easy to follow, which was a good thing. Traffic was dying down on this Monday evening, so he didn't want to get too close. As he drove, he reminded himself that tonight was only reconnaissance, *get the information you need and get out. No unnecessary risk tonight.* For a fleeting moment he couldn't tell if the thought was his, or the protective voice in his head.

Ten minutes into the journey they ended up at Police HQ. Troy wasn't surprised. In fact, he expected this was where the first leg of tonight's journey would end. Following them here would provide the piece of information he didn't have, the other detective's personal vehicle. He leered in her direction as she exited the Explorer and walked over to a matte gray Scion FR-S Coupe. It sat lower than the vehicle he had followed on the way back to the Police HQ, which significantly raised his risk. He convinced himself it didn't matter. He could follow her and avoid being seen. *How hard can it be*, he asked as he settled in two car lengths behind her at the stop light.

Troy had an answer to his question when the light turned green. The detective accelerated beyond the speed limit and didn't appear she'd be slowing down. In order to keep pace with her, he had to abandon his plan to keep cars between her and him. He pressed on the accelerator and peered down at the speedometer, 52. *What is the speed limit?* He didn't have time to find the answer to this question when he noticed the walk signal counting down. It was at three and she did not appear to be slowing down. If anything, she dropped the car into another gear so she wouldn't be caught by the light.

From his trailing position and at his current speed he would not make it to the intersection before it changed. He slammed down on the gas as he watched the signal turn from two to one. Before he passed the perpendicular crosswalk, he watched the signal reach zero. The light went from green to yellow, and then he saw the ambers of the yellow light defuse as he blew through the intersection.

He could feel his heart pumping as he looked around for any cops who may have been observing the entire situation, but he saw none. He was preparing to drop his speed until he realized the detective was doing no such thing. *What the hell is wrong with this woman?* he thought as he stayed the course. After safely bypassing two more intersections he saw the brake lights illuminate as she slowed for an already red light.

He didn't want her to get a great view of his vehicle, so he pulled into the right lane and took up behind a car already waiting. When the light changed he was thrown another curveball as she took a left. "Shit!" he exclaimed as he waited for the two cars that had pulled up behind her to drive by. He made the left from the right lane and could see she was already at least a block away. As he gave chase again, he wondered if it was worth it. *Yes,* the voice said so reluctantly he pressed on. He silently prayed that this chase would end soon, and it did so two minutes later.

Troy was still half a block away when he witnessed the Scion turn into a Home2 Suites by Hilton. He followed suit and pulled into a visitor's spot. *Okay, I know where she's staying, time to go home,* he thought as he prepared to leave. *Is that what Dillon would do?* the voice asked. In fact it was not what he'd do. He would continue to press the envelope. He would get right up next to the detective. He would have no fear. Before he could rationalize his actions any further, he was out his vehicle and standing in the lobby.

Now what? he thought, trying to blend in with the other patrons gathered in the lobby. He watched as the detective walk through the sliding doors and walked in her direction. He had the makings of a plan working as he did. She would probably need to stop by the front desk to obtain her room key. He rationalized he could stay close enough to hear both her name and her room number. At that point he could leave and take time to plan his next move.

But when she continued past the front desk, he realized his plan was deteriorating right before his eyes. He slowed his pace, reaching deep within his brain to formulate something, anything. But nothing raced to his frontal lobe, and he watched helplessly as she pressed the up button on the elevator. The light above the car read four with a down arrow next to it. It wouldn't be long before she was headed to her floor, and the night would have been a waste.

He closed his eyes, searching for another move and as if it was magic the words "Get On" appeared in white text against the black background of his shut eyelids. His eyes shot open and the ding of the elevator grounded him to the decision. Three others labored to the door as if they had too much to drink and entered the waiting car. Troy managed to slide on prior to the door closing and made his way back to the corner. He noticed floor six had been pressed, "Any other floors?" the detective asked. He thought she had a sweet voice, and it would sound even better as she pleaded to be let go.

"Five," the male said with both arms wrapped around the two women he was with. He could only imagine what was going to transpire on floor five, but he didn't want to think about it.

He still had some decisions to make. He was on the elevator as instructed, but he still didn't have a plan. He gained another piece of information. She was staying on floor six. Maybe that was the reason he was on the elevator. It was more information than he had previously. She turned and looked at him waiting on a destination and before he realized the words were coming out of his mouth he said, "Six please."

She smiled, nodded her head and turn to face the front. *What the hell!* He thought as the elevator started to climb to the designated floors. He could feel a cold sweat forming over his brow as he wondered what he'd do on floor six. He watched in a panic as the floors ticked from two to three and then three to four. It would be stopping on the next floor and when it did he only had one more floor to devise a plan. He could feel his breath growing shallow when the alert dinged. He watched as the two girls walked off the elevator followed by their mail suitor.

The doors closed and the car began to rise. He closed his eyes again, praying for another sign. When the alert dinged denoting, they were on six he realized no additional help was coming.

"After you," he said in his most disarming voice. The detective stepped off and made an immediate left and he followed. She walked as fast as she drove, which he used to his advantage. He slowed his speed but not to the point it would appear creepy. A new plan was formulating with each step. He would allow her to get to her door and simply see which room she went into. But that still didn't solve his biggest problem, what was he doing on the floor.

It didn't take long as she stopped in front of her suite. He continued to walk pass noting the room number across from where she was staying, *612*, which meant she was in 613. He casually walked past the detective eyeing the floor outside of each subsequent door. The first two rooms had a small amount of light pouring from underneath, so they were not good options. However, the third would meet his needs. He stopped at the door and knocked.

He fought the urge to turn his head to the left to see if she was watching him. Instead, he taxed his ears for two separate purposes. He needed to hear the click of the key deactivating the lock on her door, but most important he was listening for footsteps originating from behind the door in front of him. The latter happened prior to the former and he willed her to hurry. He began to calculate how much time he needed to rush to the end of the hallway to be undetected by the occupant of the room. Mercifully the sound he'd been waiting on danced to his ears. As he waited for her to walk into her room, he reminded himself, *rush but don't run*.

When the door closed behind her, he strode with purpose to the stairwell at the end of the hall. He realized the moisture in his palms as his legs propelled him forward. He heard the door unlatch behind him, but he didn't look back. He darted into the stairwell just as the door he walked away from opened. He took a deep breath and began walking down the stairs. As he did, he thought, *mission accomplished* and smiled to himself.

7

B eing a college professor was ingrained in Troy's DNA. He wasn't athletic enough for competitive sports. He wasn't smart enough to be a doctor. And he wasn't savvy enough to rub shoulders on Wall Street. His gift had always resided in his ability to convey academic concepts in a manner that made them easier to comprehend. The more complex the material, the better he performed.

In high school, while others worked at fast food joints to line their pockets, he tutored those struggling in class. He was so good at his craft that the teachers began sending him clients they felt needed the extra attention. He migrated his tutoring business with him to college, where the clientele was a bit more eclectic than that of his high school. Nonetheless he managed to help them all.

That was why he sat in his office on the second floor of Carnegie Hall dissecting what happened in lecture this morning. He struggled the entire morning connecting parallel thoughts into coherent material. His slides felt foreign since he'd become use to teaching organically as opposed to well-constructed notes. In the other areas of his life, he found the structure helped him to focus, but he never needed it in the classroom.

As he lectured, he witnessed the confused and bewildered looks from several students. He caught a few passing notes and stares back up at him as they tried to follow his train of thought. After class, the girl who sat in the second row, whose name he couldn't even recall, came to him.

"Professor Evans," she said in a concerned parental voice, "Is everything okay?"

He assured her that everything was fine, when in fact everything was completely wrong. He packed up quickly, raced to his office, shut the door behind him and dropped down into his chair. Which was exactly where he was seated at this moment trying to determine what was wrong with him.

His routine for the morning had been the same. He spent some private time with his precious daughter, Emily Ann. He had his cup of joe in the kitchen and one in his thermos. Traffic for Charlotte was lighter than normal, which made for a pleasant drive into the office. So, he was finding it increasingly impossible to pinpoint what was wrong. Then it hit him. Maybe it had nothing to do with his morning routine. Maybe it was about the activities of last night. The unbelievable risks that he took. They were completely out of character for him. Maybe it was the unnatural spikes of adrenaline from speeding down the street and running red lights. *Could the events from last night be playing havoc on my teaching?* While it seemed unlikely, it was the only rational explanation.

Sitting in his office chair psychoanalyzing himself wasn't getting him anywhere. So, he pulled out the latest assignments turned in from his class and began grading them. The first paper was from Ashleigh Sanders, *was that the name of the girl from the second row that approached me?* He shook away the thought and started reading.

The individual letters on the page morphed together until the point he saw a solid black box. He closed his eyes and shook his head in an attempt to clear his vision. When he did, the words were back on the page where they belonged, and he continued to read. The more he read, the more the paper felt like that of Mandy Cox. The structure, cadence, tone. It was as if Mandy had written the paper herself. *This isn't right*, he thought as he glared at the paper.

He started reading it again for the third time and realized it sounded nothing like Mandy. It was well-structured, thoroughly thought out, articulate, and engaging. It was everything he expected out of his students. Before the content of the paper changed on him again, he wrote "100" in the top right-hand corner and tucked the graded paper back into his bag. *One down*, he thought as someone rapped on the door.

He'd forgotten he had office hours today. He wasn't in any frame of mind to see a student, but he couldn't rightfully turn them away. He cleared his dry throat, "Come in."

The door groaned open, and Dean Franks was the first to enter followed by a woman he hadn't seen before. He began to stand so that he could greet his visitors. As he did, the voice in his head spoke with a sinister tone, *Another one.*

"Professor Evans, I'd like for you to meet Professor Mary Ludwick. She'll be teaching Intro to Creative Writing, and she's going to be your new neighbor."

The voice was back. *Look at her. The smile, the blonde hair, the doughy eyes. She basically screams I always get my way.*

"It's nice to meet you," Troy said, extending his hand to shake hers.

"The pleasure is all mine. I look forward to us being colleagues."

And listen to her voice. She'll have the entire department eating from her hand in less than a month.

"If you need anything, I'll be right next door."

"Thank you," she said.

"We have a few more stops we need to make so we'll get out of your hair." Dean Franks headed to the door followed closely by Professor Ludwick.

Troy started to feel the sensation stirring deep within him. It was the feeling that came over him when it was time to find another woman to rid the world of because of their corrupted ways. But who would it be? Before the thought could materialize in his mind, the voice spoke. *It seems to me you have two viable candidates. It's clear who Dillon would choose. The question is do you have the stones, or will you settle again for an easier prey?*

Troy knew what the voice wanted, but he wasn't sure he was ready. Something like this would be great for his next novel. It would likely catapult him to heights he hadn't seen before. Not to mention he would be ridding the world of one more loose cannon. He also knew it was outside the level of risk he felt comfortable with. But Dillon would push through, and he would make it happen. He needed to crystalize the thought in his mind. He needed to tell himself that she was the right person. If he was going after her, he'd need to know everything possible about her background.

He turned to his computer which had dropped into sleep mode. He brought it back to life and entered the password. He opened his Chrome browser and typed in Detective Elise Porter. As he waited for the results he smiled with the assurance that Dillon would have made the same decision.

8

D etectives Sampson and Porter drove the hour trip from police headquarters to Airport Rd in New London, NC, home of Albemarle Correctional Institution. Against his better judgment, Sampson agreed to pursue the useless questioning of Hugo Wolfe. Porter was convinced that Hugo would provide insight to the new murder, unaware of how wrong she was.

"With the similarities in the crime scenes, the killer and Hugo must be acquainted with each other," she argued.

Sampson planned to argue his point, but shy of concrete reasoning it would have been a losing battle. He broached the topic of her childhood again, but she expertly dodged his line of questioning by changing the topic at each turn. Before he could squeeze any answers from her, they were at the gate of the prison.

"I called ahead," Porter said, hopping out of the car. "Warden Edwards is expecting us." Sampson noticed the bounce in her step as he too stepped from the vehicle.

"If you don't mind, I'll like to start off the questioning. With the crime he's been convicted of, having to answer to a woman may throw him off his game and produce the answers we need." The typical stroll was replaced with a matter-of-fact stride, one that oozed of having a perp in the crosshairs. Sampson found he had to extend his gait to keep pace.

The guard standing post at the entrance eyed the pair curiously as they approached.

"Detectives Sampson and Porter here to see prisoner Hugo Wolfe." They both showed the guard their credentials, and he began looking through the visitor log.

"We've already cleared this visit with Warden Edwards," she said, anxious to enter.

The guard flipped the page and with his finger continued to scroll line by line. "Ah, there you are." He made a couple of entries on the paper, followed by entries on the computer. He slid the clipboard over to the detectives, "Please sign your names in the designated area."

Porter reached over and plucked the board and pen from his hands. She scribbled her name and passed it over to Sampson. "Is it possible to get a copy of the logs for anyone who visited Mr. Wolfe?"

The guard retrieved the clipboard from Sampson after he finished signing his name. "I believe you have to present the warden with a signed warrant from a judge," he said, passing them their visitor passes.

Porter looked over to Sampson, "I think we better find a judge and get the process started."

The magnetic lock to the first door disengaged, and they both walked through. They had to wait until the door they entered closed completely before the lock on the second door deactivated. Once it did, they walked through and were greeted on the other side.

Having gone through the drill before, they both stowed their firearms in the car's lockbox prior to leaving the station.

They both emptied their pockets, passed through the metal detectors, and once they were deemed to pose no threat, retrieved their belongings.

The deeper they walked into the prison, the more they sensed the changes. The air was warm and stale. The smell of lemon-scented disinfectant subtlety teased their nostrils. The vibrant colors and lush greenery surrounding the exterior of the prison had been dulled to a blue-grey tent plastering the concrete walls.

They walked past the visiting room, where murmured conversations were barely audible and longing hugs were exchanged with loved ones. Corrections officers stood by at the ready to intervene should the situation arise.

"Right this way," the guard urged, holding open a door leading toward the private visiting room. These rooms were normally reserved for inmates and their attorneys, but it was also used for detectives who wanted to question the incarcerated. They periodically staged meetings with informants when crucial details were needed, and prying eyes had to be avoided.

Sampson eyed Porter. Excitement exuded from her aura with each purposeful step she took. Her laser-focused eyes hadn't notice Sampson appraising her. She was all business and on the hunt. But she was hunting in the wrong place.

They were led to the third door on the right. Porter entered, immediately taking a seat. Sampson thanked the guard and then followed suit. The door shut behind them, and they patiently awaited the appearance of Hugo.

They didn't wait long, because two-minutes after they were seated the door from the opposite side of the room swung open. A six-foot two-inch corrections officer with a mop of black hair walked Hugo into the room.

The shackled man coming through the door was already

transitioning into a shell of the one who entered the prison a few months prior. His plump cheeks were sinking in on themselves. His ample belly had dropped a few inches. The confident gait he exhibited when Detective Sampson first met him was now an unsure shuffle. It was likely exasperated by the shackles surrounding his ankles. But the most noticeable change was his eyes.

The life that burned behind Hugo's dark brown eyes was visibly gone. It was now replaced by a flickering amber that was close to extinguishing. He hadn't been informed about who would be visiting. And when he locked eyes with Detective Sampson and then Detective Porter, the flicker transitioned to pure hatred.

The guard nudged him forward and helped him into the chair. He unlocked the cuffs, securing Hugo's hands to his waist and connected them to the metal eye located on the table. With his charge now secure, the officer backed into the corner, where he would be a silent observer keeping an eye on his prisoner.

"What do you want?" Hugo asked. His voice strained with each word as he glared holes into each of them.

"How are the accommodations?" Porter asked.

His eyebrows stitched together while he determined how he'd answer the question. "Shitty, thanks to you."

"Great," she said cracking a smile. "You're getting exactly what a depraved psychopath should. But it can get much worse. Once we tie you to the most recent victim, it will."

He slammed his hands on the table and quickly jumped to his feet. "Most recent victim! I never had any victim, you stupid–"

Before the words could tumble from his lips, the guard forced him back down into his chair. "I've already warned you once, Hugo. Another outburst like that and it'll be the hole for you."

He dropped his head into his hands. When he spoke, the despair resonated in his voice. "I told you before that I had nothing to do with the death of Mandy. But you refused to listen. And now you walk in here trying to pin another murder on me. What a fucking joke. I've been locked up in this hell hole. How exactly would I have committed this new murder?"

"I'm so glad you asked," Porter responded. "It appears a copycat is out there picking up where you left off. It stands to reason you told someone about the details of your crime."

"I didn't tell anyone about any crime, because I didn't do this. Are you even listening?"

"Or that's exactly what you want us to believe. If there is someone out there committing these atrocities in the same manner, then you can continue this charade of innocence."

"That's because I am innocent!" he yelled, jumping from his seat. Before the guard could move, he dropped back into his chair.

"Has it ever dawned on you that the person who committed this latest murder is the one who committed the first one?"

"No," she said flatly. "In fact, each night I sleep in my bed, I'm thankful you have been taken off the street. Furthermore, we will obtain a log of those who have visited you. I'm sure we'll find the person responsible."

Hugo let out a guttural laugh. "Well, knock yourself out. From the moment that guilty verdict was rendered, my family has disowned me. I haven't had one visitor. Not one. So, you go ahead and pull your list and then you'll likely start to believe me."

Sampson, who had been quiet during the exchange, spoke up. "If not you, then who?"

Porter's head snapped in the direction of her partner.

"Don't you think I have asked myself that question every day since you came to my home and arrested me? I wish I knew, but I don't have a clue. I admit I had a sexual relationship with her, and it was not my finest moment, but I did not kill her."

Sampson pressed, "Is there anyone that had an ax to grind with you and thus would set you up to take the fall for this crime?"

Porter shot daggers in his direction, and he ignored each one.

"No. No one. Don't you think I would have offered this information if I had it?"

"Then who are you working with?" Porter asked with venom dripping from each word.

"You really don't listen, do you? I've already told you, I... did...not...kill...her! You're simply barking up the wrong tree. If there has been another murder, the more time you spend looking into me, the longer it will take you to find the killer."

Sampson knew he was correct. This questioning was a waste of time, and as he expected Hugo didn't have any answers. Porter peppered him with questions for another ten minutes. She grew increasingly frustrated with each answer as she figured he was hiding the truth. And Hugo's frustration came from his innocence that was falling on deaf ears.

Once they concluded their session with Hugo, they were led back to the entrance. The minute they stepped out into the warm Charlotte day, Porter entered Sampson's personal space.

"What the hell was that?"

"Badgering Hugo with questions about an accomplice was getting us nowhere. So I changed tactics to see if we could get information another way."

Porter was about to follow-up when a question came from

over her shoulder, "Detectives, we saw you at the crime scene yesterday, and now you're here at the penitentiary. Could this have anything to do with Hugo Wolfe? If you are visiting Hugo, does that mean he is innocent? Something he has continued to say from day one."

The short, red-headed reporter shoved her mic between the detectives while her cameraman filmed the interaction. While they tried to keep the details of the latest murder a secret, some of the information had leaked.

Porter was quick to respond, "We have not made any determinations on the case at this point. We simply made the trip here to follow a line of inquires."

"So, there is a chance you have the wrong man in custody?"

Instead of answering the question, Porter made a state-ment. "We are at the early stages of our investigation. What we know without a shadow of a doubt is that the individual we are dealing with is deranged. Anyone who preys on the inno-cent is evil. But to do what he is doing to these young women is deplorable. We will overturn ever rock until this person is locked away."

"So does that mean this person is a copycat?"

Sampson had enough and said, "We really need to get back to work. Thank you all." He began walking in the direc-tion of the car, and Porter followed on his heels. As if it wasn't already bad enough, the press had begun sneaking around. This was just one more headache he didn't have time to deal with. Instead of focusing on them and Hugo, he shifted his thoughts to how he'd track down the real killer.

9

There's no other place in the world Troy Evans would want to be than with his beautiful wife and their amazing little girl. But on this night, while his body was present, his thoughts were elsewhere. He could feel his psyche pulling against itself within these worlds he lived in. On the one hand, he was an attentive and present husband and father. The unconditional love he felt from his family grounded him to reality.

Bethany's affectionate caress when he passed her in the bedroom as they prepared to turn in for the night. The gentle kiss she planted on his cheek each morning as he rushed out the door. The thoughtful text in the middle of the day to say, "I'm thinking about you." It was all real. Something he could touch, feel, sense.

The way Emily smiled when she heard his voice. When she sensed him nearby, she was already doing her best to push her legs against the ground so she could make her way to him. When he read her bedtime stories, she nestled in the bend of his arm doing everything she could to be close to her daddy. Again, real. Tangible.

But there was another side. A darker side. It was the side where what was real hinged on the verge of being a figment of his imagination. It was the side where the personalities of the main character and the author merged into a single unit and the fiction became reality. Dillon was no longer the character on the pages. He was now fused with Troy. They were for all intents and purposes the same person.

So while Troy the dutiful husband and father sat at the dinner table enjoying a home cooked meal, Dillon paced anxiously in his mind waiting for his turn at the wheel. He willed his host to conclude the meal, walk into his home office, and plan the next hunt. Troy managed to keep Dillon at bay, but with each word written in their shared novel, Dillon edged Troy closer and closer to the corner.

"That's a good girl," Bethany said to Emily as she consumed the last ounce of milk. "That should help you sleep through the night." She turned and looked at Troy, "Did you enjoy dinner? It's not like you to be so quiet."

"It was delicious. I can't take another bite. And sorry I wasn't much company this evening. Just a lot on my mind." He pulled the napkin from his lap, folded it, and dropped it in the center of his plate. "I was just thinking that I need to change my midterm exam. One of my students from last year posted the answers online. Another faculty member brought it to my attention, so now I will need to rewrite the whole thing."

"Kids these days," she said, wiping Emily's mouth. "They will do anything they can to circumvent the system. But one thing is for sure...they will not outsmart my witty husband." She leaned over to give him a kiss on the cheek and a quick rub on his shoulder. "I'm going to take Emily up for a bath and then lay her down for the night. I think I'll turn in early too. I've been tired all day."

She maneuvered their daughter from her highchair and

leaned her in so she could give Troy a kiss. Afterward, she grabbed what she needed for the night and said, "You're on dishes."

Troy smile in her direction and said, "Can't we just buy new ones?"

She shot him a glance and he relented, "Okay, I'll take care of them." He watched as the two girls that meant everything to him headed up the stairs.

Loading the dishwasher took fifteen minutes, and with that task now done Troy walked in the direction of his office. With each step, he could feel Dillon pushing his way to the forefront. He sat in his chair, pulled the laptop from his bag, and fired it up. He had student's papers to grade before class tomorrow, but they had to wait. Dillon was now in control, and with the time he spent pacing during dinner he had formulated a plan.

He opened his Chrome browser window and typed in Elise Porter. The results raced to the screen. Over ten million results in 0.66 seconds. He thought, *who knew there were so many people with the same name.* He narrowed the search by typing in Elise Porter North Carolina. He recalled reading somewhere she had ties to the state, so he hoped this would yield better results

More than seven million results in 0.49 seconds. Still too many results to sift through. He decided on one more search, Detective Elise Porter North Carolina. This time one million results came back in 0.80 seconds. But the numbers were irrelevant, because right there as the first result sat a picture of the detective. He clicked the link and began to read. By the time he was done, he had jotted down some key notes.

- Elise Porter attended Appalachian State University in Boone, North Carolina

- She majored in criminology with a minor in psychology
- She completed her undergraduate degree in five years with a 3.2 GPA
- She applied for the police academy less than a year after completing her degree
- She graduated the academy ranked eighth in her class of fifteen
- She was on the force four years before applying to become a detective
- She recently transferred to the CMPD

TROY GLARED AT HIS NOTES. He wanted to derive meaning from the information he gathered, but there wasn't much there. However, there were two threads he wanted to tug on a bit more.

It took the detective five years to complete her degree. Yes, she had a minor, but the coursework alone could have been completed in four years given the GPA she received. Therefore, there was likely a reason for the additional year, something this press release didn't share or didn't know. *Could this be a hidden skeleton in our closet, Ms. Porter?*

The answer to his question would manifest in the second thread. Throughout his academic studies, Troy had the opportunity to meet numerous educators. Some were employed at various high schools around the country, while others were professors teaching at institutions of higher learning. One such person was Patrick Lentz.

. . .

PATRICK AND TROY were roommates their first year in college. Like Troy, Patrick was not a native North Carolinian. He had grown up in Texas where his family had a cattle business. He didn't want to join it and preferred to venture out on his own. When it came time to select a university to continue his education, he spun a map of the United States on his table. Before it came to a stop, he closed his eyes and stabbed his finger into the spinning paper. His finger landed on North Carolina. He began looking into the various colleges, and as he always said, "The rest is history."

While they'd come from different backgrounds, the two got along well for two strangers living together. Troy was an English major who struggled with college math, whereas Patrick was a math major who struggled with English. They made a pact to help one another survive freshman year, and that's exactly what they did.

Although they parted ways at the end of the year, they scarcely stayed in contact. Troy was surprised on graduation day to be seated behind his former roommate for the commencement ceremonies. Troy mentioned he was still on the hunt to land a teaching gig, while Patrick mentioned he secured a teaching assistant position for a college in Boone. They wished each other well and ended their college career how they ended their freshman year, by parting ways.

When Bethany and Troy decided they'd move back to North Carolina, Troy reached out to his former roommate, who was now the admissions counselor at Appalachian State University. Patrick apologized profusely that they didn't have any open positions but recommended Troy to UNCC who had an immediate opening.

. . .

Now as Troy reviewed the bulleted list he created from what he currently knew about the detective, he typed out an email to Patrick. In his correspondence, he asked his friend to do him a favor and provide anything he could about a former student. Troy had enough of the computer for the evening, so he clicked on the TV. He immediately went in search of the news. His need for the hunt was not quenched, so he wanted to feed his high with the perfect crime that dominated the airwaves. He changed the channel to the local CBS affiliate, and to his surprise there she was on the screen, Detective Elise Porter. Sampson stood next to her with a perturbed expression on his face. He quickly surveyed the surroundings and realized they were outside a penitentiary. *Visiting Mr. Wolfe, I presume.* He increased the volume and caught the tail end of the interview.

"We are at the early stages of our investigation. What we know without a shadow of a doubt is that the individual we are dealing with is deranged. Anyone who preys on the innocent is evil. But to do what he is doing to these young women is deplorable. We will overturn ever rock until this person is locked away."

Dillon's voice was loud in clear in his head. *She doesn't respect us. In fact, she mocks our very existence. There will be no more debate—she is the one. Think how great the story will be. The cop who hunts the killer is now the one being hunted. Just imagine how your fans will eat up this story.*

Troy found himself nodding to each word Dillon spoke.

Why don't we have a little fun while we're at it? Let's see if we can get Detective Sampson to play along.

Deep in the recesses of his mind, a piece of Troy wordlessly yelled, *This is a bad idea!* But no one cared to listen. Troy retrieved the burner phone tucked away in his work bag and dialed the number he had for Sampson. It only took three rings for him to answer.

"It's a shame, Detective, you were unable to save Brianna, but that just means you have another opportunity to succeed."

He listened as Sampson lobbed threats, but he would not be deterred.

"It's simple. I will give you clues about the victim before she has been taken. If you can figure out who she'll be, consider yourself a hero. But should you fail again, Detective, that's another death that will be on your hands."

He grew bored listening to Sampson's drivel about how he would catch him and make him pay. He interrupted, "Whether you agree to play or not, that's totally up to you. But I'll tell you this, you'll regret not playing when you realize you had everything you needed to save this poor woman. Nonetheless, here is the first clue. Objects in this mirror are closer than they appear."

He disconnected the call and turned off the TV. Dillon's voice spoke loud and clear. *The hunt is on again.*

10

T he smell of lavender from the burning candles permeated the bathroom in room 613 at the Home2 Suites hotel. The steam from the shower poured over its enclosure into the spacious room, fogging the mirror in the process. Porter made it a ritual to wash away the day the minute she stepped into her home, a practice she carried with her to these temporary accommodations.

After their visit to the jail and a couple of interviews, Porter kept her promise and met with her realtor. The first property had potential, but she worried about the pearl-white carpet covering every inch of the split-level home. The realtor rationalized if she didn't like the carpet, she could always pull it up, but in her mind while it didn't work for her it would likely be a welcome sight for another home seeker. Furthermore, it looked new, so tearing up that hard work didn't make sense to her. She promised to keep it as an option pending the other locations.

The second home felt too perfect. It had everything she was looking for, three bedrooms, a luxurious kitchen, and best of all a loft that she could turn into a home gym. She loved the size of the yard, and it felt right. She tried to objectively look at the other two home visits that were planned, but she thought she found the one. She stated she wanted to sleep on it for a night and review each one. Her realtor gave her the comps for each location and advised her not to think on it too long. The market was hot, and someone could pluck it right from underneath her.

As the water beat on the back of her neck and traced down her spine, she thought about the different properties. While they were all nice, the second one was the one that was right for her. She stepped from the shower with her mind made up. She would contact Tracy in the morning with her decision and get the ball rolling.

She quickly dried her hair and then wrapped herself in the towel. She gave the mirror a couple of swipes and grabbed her electric toothbrush from the charger. The excitement of purchasing a new home in her new city took her back to her childhood when she shared a bathroom with her siblings.

"COME ON, Elise. I need to brush my teeth so I can go to bed." Edward, her six-year-old younger brother banged on the door again, but it remained locked. This was the third time this week she'd taken twenty minutes showering and preparing for bed, but tonight he had a surprise for her. He prepared to bang again when he heard the loose handle jiggle and the door creak open.

He was caught off guard and had to scurry before the door opened fully. When it did, he unleashed a full squeeze of the super soaker water gun he received for Christmas the previous year. Elise squealed as the cold water plastered her clothes and her skin.

"You little–" She began chasing him down the hallway into

the room that they shared. Edward jumped onto his bed, trapped with nowhere to go. "You are going to pay for that, you rascal."

She began tickling him on his side, and he screamed out with laughter, "Stop! Stop! Uncle! I give. I give."

"Oh, you give. I think not!" She pulled the super soaker from the bed, cocked it once, and squeezed. The stream of cold water shot from the barrel and connected with his helpless body. He howled at the top of his lungs until he was out of breath.

"You kids, stop all that noise," their mother yelled from downstairs.

They broke into instant laughter, and Elise flopped down onto the bed. When the laughter subsided, Edward had a serious look on his face.

"What's wrong, Eddy," she asked, shifting onto her elbow. She watched as the gears ground in his head. She couldn't tell if he was trying to figure out what to say, or if he knew what he wanted to say but didn't want to say it.

"What's going to happen when..." he bit his lip and cast his eyes to the far away wall.

"When what?" she implored.

He started differently. "Will we still be close like – this when the baby arrives?"

She smiled, "Of course we will, silly. Why would you ask that?"

"What if you like the new baby more than you like me?"

She thought about it for a minute and then said, "Maybe you are right, especially if he or she doesn't spray me with water guns."

His head shot up ready to protest, but before he could she said, "I'm kidding! We'll always be close no matter what."

Hope sprung into his eyes, "You promise?"

"I promise."

He leaned over and hugged her, and she returned the gesture.

RECALLING this memory brought a tear to her eye, because she had not kept her promise to him. While it wasn't the new baby who came between them, she did allow events later in their childhood to pull them apart. She tried to clear the thought from her mind, because it was at times too painful to bear. She often wondered what it would have been like if she kept her promise. Would he be here with her now, living in Charlotte? She had no way of knowing, and she couldn't go back and change the past.

She finished brushing her teeth and moved into the bedroom. There she finished toweling off and rummaged through her suitcase for a new pair of pajamas. With the top and bottom matching set in hand, she dressed and tossed the towel on the corner of the bed.

She walked over to the window and pulled back a corner of the drapes. Although the night was settling in, she could still spot the tell-tale signs of a storm brewing. She walked back across the room, sat in the chair at the desk, and pondered the case.

She couldn't get past the manner in which Sampson had behaved during the conversation with Hugo. It was almost as if he didn't share her convictions on the case. Partners didn't agree 100 percent of the time, but she felt it was more than that. His standoffish demeanor he had with the press. The way he circumvented her line of questioning. There was something there, but she didn't know what.

In that moment, she decided to keep a closer eye on him. She chided herself for feeling that her new partner of two days was hiding something from her, but as a detective she learned to live off her gut feeling, and in this case it was telling her he was hiding something.

The thoughts of her brother, and the doubt of her partner was souring her mood. She picked up her phone, found the number she was searching for, and set out to type a text message.

It was short and to the point, "I've made a decision. Let's discuss first thing in the morning." Once the message was sent, she smiled again thinking about the new home that would soon be hers.

11

B efore the sun rose over the horizon, Sampson was seated at his desk pecking away at the keyboard. Last night's exchange with the killer took root in his psyche and began to fester. The killer made it painfully obvious he'd already identified his new victim. Although Sampson flatly refused to play his sadistic game, once the killer uttered the first clue he had Sampson hooked.

SAMPSON TRIED TO SLEEP, but how could he? The killer was already one step ahead. After an hour spent tossing and turning, he knew sleep would elude him. He flung the already tangled sheet to the other side of his king-size bed and devised an action plan.

First on the agenda was cardio and weights. He knew if he didn't expend the excess energy coursing through his system, he would be unable to focus. Luckily for Sampson, the gym was in the next room. He ran five miles on the treadmill, increasing both the speed and the incline with each mile. He focused his mind on his breathing and the cadence in his stride. If his mind drifted back to the case, he admonished himself with another tick in the acceleration. By the time he concluded his run, he achieved his fastest five miles since the academy. *Guess I thought about the case more than I realized.*

Satisfied with his cardio efforts, he stepped over to his adjustable dumbbells. He consulted his planned workout regimen for the day and immediately dove into it. The penalty for thinking about the case would be an additional five pounds. Unlike his efforts on the treadmill, he kept his mental discipline and only allowed one thought to creep in. Once he was done, he stowed away the equipment and headed to the shower.

SAMPSON EYED the clock in the corner of his monitor and realized that had been six hours ago. He reached for his coffee mug, disgusted by the stale smell and pungent taste, but it served a critical need, caffeine. He hadn't bothered to brew a pot since 4:00 a.m., and it certainly tasted like it. Instead, he spent time focusing on the cryptic clue, *objects in this mirror are closer than they appear.*

He searched the internet looking for an obscure second meaning. He found pages of useless entries that in no way aided his investigation. On a whim, he researched cases in which a mirror was used as a weapon. He fully expected zero hits and was shocked to find four. He carefully read each case only to come up empty once again. For hours he racked his brain trying to derive meaning, and with each dead end his frustration grew.

He closed his eyes and pinched the bridge of his nose, feeling he'd exhausted all options, but he knew he couldn't give up. A young girl's life was at stake, and he would not fail her. *Not like Brianna.* A disturbance within his vicinity caused him to open his eyes. Porter had arrived, and she carried in her hands two dozen donuts from Duck Donuts, and even better than that she had two cups of coffee.

She sat the boxes in the common area and began walking toward Sampson. He quickly killed the crime database as she turned the corner and handed him the cup. Steam rose from the cup carrying along the smell of hazelnut. He said, "You are a saint."

She appraised him and said, "You look like shit. How long have you been here?"

He'd been sitting at his desk so long it hadn't dawned on him how he might look to others. "A couple hours," he lied, greedily drinking from the cup. "Thanks for the coffee. It's just what the doctor ordered."

He sensed her eyeing him wearily, but she didn't immediately say anything. Before she could articulate the thought she'd been conjuring, he made his way to the sweets. The best thing about their donuts was that they made them fresh and to order. Not to mention the unbelievable flavors they concocted. He reached for his favorite, Chocolate Carmel Crunch, and a napkin.

"Great call," he said, taking a large bite.

"Nothing like a donut to start the day. So, did you find any new leads?"

"Not exactly. But the phone records, including text messages, that you ordered finally arrived. I figured we'd divide and conquer."

"Sounds like as good of plan as any. Which one do you want, phone records or text?"

"I'll take the phone records. I'm certain I don't want to delve into the mind of a teenage girl."

"Chicken," she said with a smile while turning to her desk.

Before she could sit down, the captain yelled out, "Sampson. Porter. My office, now." They eyed each other and then shrugged their shoulders. Sampson took one last gigantic bite of his donut that should have probably been two and they made their way to his office.

As they filed in, Marshall sat behind his desk rhythmically tapping his pen. Before they grabbed a seat, he asked, "Where are we with the Brianna case?"

Porter was first to her chair and first to speak, "We visited Hugo Wolfe at the prison yesterday. We asked him who he's been working with prior to his incarnation or after. It's clear he knows the person responsible. We also asked the judge to grant us a warrant so we can see who has visited him. He claims he's had no visitors, but the records may tell a different story. I'm sure if we squeeze him hard enough, he'll give up his accomplice."

"Unless it wasn't him," Sampson said, drawing their attention. "If Wolfe is innocent like he's been claiming since his arrest, then the killer is not a copycat or an accomplice. He is simply the killer."

"Just one second," Marshall boomed with furrowed brows. "It was the two of you who captured him with solid detective work. It was the two of you who testified to the authenticity of the evidence at his hearing. The one in which a jury of his peers took less than an hour to find him guilty on all charges."

He fixed Sampson with a cold glare. "Now you're sitting in my office asserting his innocence. That's some balls on you, if I say so myself. Do you have any proof of his innocence?"

From his peripheral vision, he could see his partner's body language change and could sense her fury for not backing her idea. In that moment he thought about coming clean.

He could inform them of the call he received immediately following Hugo's arrest. He could tell them about the agonizing week he spent trying to find Brianna just to come up short. He'd lay it all on the line by alerting them to the clue he received and the more clues to come about the next victim. But what would that gain him?

He still didn't have any proof of Hugo's innocence. He didn't have a clue to the killer's identity. The only thing he had was his pride, and if he was being honest it was his ego.

He'd been bested by the killer once, and his ego wouldn't allow him to ask for help. No, he had to see this through. He had to beat the killer at his own game. Even if that meant deceiving both his boss and his partner.

"No, I don't have any proof," he answered.

"I've told you before, we can't convict on a hunch. If there isn't anything to exonerate Hugo of the crime he's been convicted for, then don't bring it back up. Assume he's always been working with someone, or he's managed to convince someone to pick up where he left off. I don't want this turning into a circus, and I want this case brought to a speedy conclusion. Is that clear?"

"Absolutely, sir. Crystal clear," Porter responded.

Sampson didn't respond immediately so Marshall lowered his tone, "Is that clear, Detective?"

"Point taken," he responded.

"Good. Now go find this psychopath before he strikes again."

Outside Marshall's office, Porter laid into Sampson. "Just what in the hell was that, Carl? Partners are supposed to have each other's back, and I have this feeling that you're going against everything I suggest."

"Elise, our job is to ensure we catch the right perp. Even if that means we made a mistake in the beginning. We're in the wrong if we turn a blind eye to other alternatives."

"Alternatives? Do you have one to substantiate your

claim?" He could feel her eyes cutting through him. "Well, do you?"

"Not at this moment."

"Then like the boss said, let it go until you do. Until then we follow this line."

Sampson's phone rang. He answered.

"This is Sampson."

"Carl, glad I caught you," Brandy said. "Can you stop by my office? I found something I think you need to see."

"We can be there in thirty." Porter shot him an inquisitive glance.

"Good. I'll see you then."

She disconnected the call, and Sampson placed his phone back into his pocket.

"Brandy's found something related to our case. We should get going." He started off in the direction of his desk.

"We'll pick this up later," she said, following on his heels.

12

The morning went how Troy imagined it would. He apologized profusely for not having the latest assignment ready to return. As a bonus, he gave the students an extra week to prepare for the next exam. This was met with a mummer of cheers and applauds from those assembled. With that out of the way, he proceeded into the scheduled lecture and breezed through the remainder of class.

Now as he sat in his office, door askew in case a student stopped by for office hours, he pondered his next move. He'd already provided Sampson with the first clue. It was obscure enough to get his juices flowing but didn't have enough detail to provide him an answer. For this plan of his to succeed, he needed additional details. He needed to hear from Patrick.

He arrived early enough this morning to drop off some items in his office. He also checked for a message from his former roommate. He hadn't heard anything yet. But he rationalized it was late last night when he sent the message and early this morning when he checked for a response. He simply had to provide him some time to research and respond.

However, in these high-stake games he was playing, timing was the key.

He logged into his laptop and opened his email client. He scrolled beyond the promotional items occupying space in his inbox. Midway down the second page, he found what he was searching for, an email from Patrick with an attachment.

HEY, Troy. It's good to hear from you, buddy. It's been way too long since we last caught up. I heard that beautiful wife of yours was pregnant with your first child. If memory serves me correctly the little one should be here now. Look at you, you lucky dog. Prettiest girl at the university and now a baby. Hopefully fatherhood treats you well. Hey, let's not go this long without hearing from each other again. I'd love to catch up.

Anyway, I pulled the records for Elise Porter, and you'll find it attached. I knew the name sounded familiar, and then I recall the paper she wrote for her English class. It was the talk of my staff for a couple weeks. I've included that as well.

Again, it was good hearing from you. Don't forget, let's connect soon.

THE TALK of my staff for a couple weeks, Troy thought. Something that powerfully written piqued his curiosity. He located the attachment, opened it, and read.

I HONESTLY THINK writing is a waste of time. I'm only taking this class because it's a required part of the curriculum to ensure I'm a well-rounded student by the time I graduate. While I appreciate the intent, that's not what I care about at this moment. I care about this incessant rage that racing though every fiber of my being.

It's now been three weeks since the death of my father. Who am I kidding? I'm being kind calling it a death. It's more like a slow suicide from what the company he worked his whole life for did to him.

Last year my dad was an excited, and if you will, well-rounded individual. He'd raise the three of us and adored my mom. He was a mere four years from retirement and receiving his full pension. I still feel the pain in my mother's words when she called to tell me what happened.

I was walking across campus after exiting my Psych 100 class when my phone rang. I answered to hear my normally stoic mom frantic on the other end. The CEO of my dad's company had secretly been embezzling money from the pension plan. Something he'd been doing for years. The feds caught wind that something shady had been going down. All signs pointed to the chief financial officer finding the discrepancies between the account and the ledger. Before he could be arrested, he drained the remainder of the account and took off overseas to a country that doesn't have an extradition treaty with the US.

My dad was devastated. He didn't have any other form of financial planning other than his pension. While retirement wouldn't be an issue because of my mom's job, we will get to her in a minute, it was the principal of the matter.

My father put all his trust and hard work into a company only to have them betray him. He went on a downhill spiral after that. He began drinking every day, something he'd never done before this incident. He did it to numb away the pain, but the pain never left.

Three weeks ago, nearly a year after this whole ordeal, he'd been on another one of his benders at the pub. Witnesses say he lost his balance on the edge of the curb when he stumbled into the street and was struck by a passing truck. He was rushed to the hospital, where he lay fighting for his life. When my mother called, I dropped everything, jumped in my car with nothing but the clothes on my back, and began speeding back home. The university was one hundred and fifty miles from my house, and I prayed I would make it. But I didn't.

Thirty minutes into my drive she called back to tell me he was gone. My heart stopped beating, and I lost control of all motor functions. My car began to veer taking up multiple lanes when I regained control. I safely pulled over to the side and cried. I cried for the loss of my father, who taught me how to be strong. I grieved because he didn't deserve this end. The tears flowed because I wasn't there to comfort him like he had done for me countless times before.

But you see, that's not all. In the Porter household there's a tale more damning than that. It took place in high school, junior year.

From the time our youngest sister Emma was born, there was a change in my brother, Edward. It started off small with him hiding the baby bottles during feeding time. He always got the biggest laugh when we searched the house for them. No one else in the house thought it was funny, especially my mom.

I pulled my little brother aside and told him it wasn't cool, and he needed to cut it out before he got into serious trouble. He simply shrugged his shoulders and went on about his day.

Then there was this one time we were at my aunt's house. I was headed back from the bathroom when I saw Edward sneaking out of her room. I didn't think anything of it at the time. Two days later, I was helping my mom with dinner when she called. She was upset because she couldn't find the locket their mom had given her before she passed away. She said the last place she had it was in her room on her dresser. She had not put it away with the rest of her jewelry when she took it off because she was rushing for our visit. My gut told me what happened to it, and I hoped I was wrong.

While my brother was outside with his friends, I excused myself from dinner preparations and marched straight to Edward's room. It took some digging around, but in between his mattress and box spring I located the missing locket. My heart sank to think he could steal something so precious from our aunt. I placed it back where I found it and went back to complete the dinner prep.

Later that evening, I confronted him about it and told him he had to come clean. He just stared at me with a hollow gaze and said he didn't see what the big deal was. He saw it, he liked it, so he took it. Our conversation turned into raised voices, which prompted my mom to come see what the fuss was about. When she saw the necklace in his hand, she gasped. She stormed into the room and yanked it from his hand.

The tongue lashing he received didn't seem to have any effect on him whatsoever. My mom, a trained psychiatrist by the way, stopped yelling midway through and just looked at him. For his part, he looked back at her with the same hollow expression he displayed with me earlier.

He continued to rack up one incident after another until my mom had enough, and this spelled the beginning of the end.

She started procedures to have him institutionalized. She said his behaviors were classic symptoms of antisocial personality disorder. She said it was the best thing for him and the only way to keep him from being an imminent threat to himself and others. My father fought it, and I fought it, but in the end she won out. Even when they took him away, he looked as if he didn't have a care in the world, a look that haunts me to this day.

So, you see, I don't really care about being a well-rounded individual at this point, because the pain I feel and how I get through it is the only thing that matters to me at this moment. But I will say this, writing this has been therapeutic, because now that I've gotten it off my chest I will never speak of it again.

WELL, a father who commits suicide and a brother locked away in a mental institution. That's quite the impressive family you have there, Detective Porter. But what else are you hiding? He scanned the remainder of what had been sent to him, but his mind drifted back to the paper. A plan had begun to materialize, and he grinned to himself once it was clear in his mind.

"It's time I pay Mr. Edward Porter a visit. "

13

Sampson and Porter traveled across town to the ME's office. The only words exchanged were, "Can we lower the AC temperature?" with a response in the affirmative. Sampson recognized the mistake he was making by not bringing his partner in on everything he knew. He sensed the impact it was having on their relationship as partners. He'd give himself until they arrived at their destination to hatch a plan to turn things around. And if he couldn't, he'd simply come clean with what he knew, all of it.

He saw their target building drawing near with each revolution of the car's tires. Meanwhile his brain was spinning with ideas, yet none of them seemed right. He began stringing together thoughts at random to meet his stated goal, and by the time they pulled into the parking lot, he had settled on a plan.

He stilled himself as they stepped out into the muggy Charlotte weather. "Elise, let me apologize. The re-emergence of this crime in this fashion is impacting me more than I could have imagined. Why don't we agree to meet halfway? I'm willing to concede it could be someone working with Hugo, if you are willing to consider we may have arrested the wrong man. Let's look at it from both points of view. You'll be my devil's advocate, and I'll be yours. This way we are running with parallel options and widening our perspectives."

She didn't immediately respond. She only wordlessly stared at him. Finally, after interminable silence she said, "We'll play this your way, Sampson, as long as you play fair."

Sampson pondered the request prior to agreeing. Once the agreement was made, a truce had been entered. The pair continued to the building in search for the ME's office.

Porter commented, "I've always hated walking in on an autopsy. The gaseous smells from a body during decomposition causes havoc on my gag reflex," She contorted her face as if she was recalling the smell from memory.

Sampson dug deep into his pocket, retrieved a small cylindrical item, and tossed it underhanded to her. She snatched it from the air, regarding it with a quizzical look. "Vapor Rub?"

"Dab a little under your nostrils, and you won't smell a thing. You'll thank me later." Their search came to an end when they reached the exterior of the ME's office. Sampson turned the handle and Porter quickly smeared the gelatinous substance under her nose.

"Whatcha got for us, Doc," he said, entering the office. He soon realized the person standing at the examining table wasn't the ME. It was her assistant, Charles. Sampson had only ran into the assistant on two occasions, and during each interaction he felt something was a little off about him. Dr. Brown swore he was brilliant and would one day run his own office. Secretly Sampson was hoping that day would come sooner than later so he didn't have to interact with him any longer.

"Hey, Charles," he said, recovering. "Where's Brandy?"

In his nasally robotic voice he said, "Dr. Brown stepped

out. She'll return momentarily." He then gazed as if viewing something from a distance. Sampson resisted the urge to turn for as long as he could, but the curiosity got the best of him. He slowly turned to look over his right shoulder. He quickly realized the strained look that had overcome their host.

Instead of a dab of Vapor Rub under each nostril, Porter opted for a finger full. The caked-on substance had shone brightly against the lights in the office. Sampson turned back to Charles and said, "This is my new partner, Elise Porter. Elise, this is Charles. One of the best ME assistants in the area. Soon to have his own office."

Porter took two steps forward, and the two shook hands, "It's a pleasure to meet you."

"The pleasure's all mine."

Without warning, the door opened behind them followed by the entrance of Dr. Brandy Brown.

"Sampson, Porter. Thank you for coming so quickly. Charles, I just received a call that a corpse floated to shore at Lake Norman. Can you handle it while I speak with the detectives?"

"Absolutely, Dr. Brown. I'll head there now." He turned on his heels, obtained his belongings, and walked out the door.

Dr. Brown motioned for the two detectives to follow her as she walked in the direction of the corpse covered on the table.

"I completed my autopsy of Brianna Armstrong. If there is any consolation, she had not been sexually assaulted, but I'm afraid that's where the good news ends. Although her skin has been expertly removed, there are indentions around the wrist and ankles signifying she had been restrained. By the depth of the wounds, I'm confident the victim was alive while this was happening to her."

From the corner of his eye, Sampson sensed Porter shift her weight.

"It's also clear to me that the victim put up a fight. I found skin cells under the nail on her middle finger of her right hand. The scratch she made was deep enough to draw blood, some of which was still attached to the skin sample. I've already ran it for DNA, and it's not a match to our victim which means –"

"That it's a match to our suspect," Sampson said. "Tell me you were able to identify who he is."

"I ran the sample through every database, and our suspect is not in there. That means he's either new at this life of crime or is very meticulous."

"There has to be a way to identify him," Porter said.

"Of course there is. You find me a suspect; I match the DNA. Other than that, I'm afraid there aren't many other options."

"Great, now all we must do is find a male with a scar somewhere on his body. That really narrows the list," Porter said sarcastically.

Sampson eyed her wearily, because where she saw an insurmountable obstacle he saw a glimmer of hope. It was just one more clue in his bag that would help him find the son of a bitch.

"Thank you, Brandy, for all your assistance. If you find anything else, let us know."

"Will do."

He nudged Porter, "Let's go. We have a killer to find."

14

The temperature gauge inside the AC-cooled vehicle read 92 degrees. Troy watched the heat from the sun generate condensation across the pavement. The voices in his head convinced him this was where he needed to be, but his body had yet to comply with the command to open the door and exit.

From the moment the voices became ever-present in his mind, he'd taken more chances. Riskier chances. Yet with each one of them, he felt he had some semblance of control. But the mission he was on today verged on the side of reckless and not a well-thought through plan. Nonetheless, he found himself here, waiting.

He told himself he would exit the vehicle at 11:00 a.m. But when the time came, his brain could not convince his hand to grasp the handle and pull. He decided he would wait fifteen minutes and this time there would be nothing stopping him from proceeding. But as the minutes changed from fourteen to fifteen, he found himself paralyzed from taking action. He talked himself into two more fifteen-minute reprieves, and with each one he found another reason to stay seated.

Now as he looked at the clock, two minutes until noon, he knew he was running out of time if he planned to act today. And if he didn't act today, he decided he would not come back again. So, it was simple, act in the next two minutes or abandon the plan he had already put into motion. He knew Dillion would not have been pondering this notion. He would have arrived, stepped out of the car, did what he needed to do, and would be at home relaxing. Ten minutes tops. But he already wasted more than an hour sitting in this same spot, willing himself to act.

He looked at the time on the dashboard, *11:59*, and before he knew it, the handle was in his hand. He pulled back, releasing the latch, and the door swung open. The cool air that had been trapped in the vehicle with him for the last hour was rudely displaced by the stifling heat and humidity.

But it didn't matter because as quickly as the heat barged into the vehicle, he was out of his seat, closing the door and walking. He reminded himself it was important to look casual. He didn't need to draw any attention to himself. If we walked like he belonged there, no one would question it.

He watched as an elderly couple exited the building. They both greeted him with a smile, and the man held the door for him.

"Thank you, sir," he said as he walked through the door and into the lobby. The staff at the counter of the Home2-Suites were busy checking in customers and paid him little attention. Which was a bonus, because he didn't want to be on their radar anyway. He didn't want anyone to recall his appearance. He recognized the smell of fresh tulips mixed with stale coffee wafting through the air.

Now that he was in the building, it was important to work quickly. He walked to the elevator and decided he would catch it up to the seventh floor. He tapped his pocket to ensure the device was secured in his pocket.

Unlike the first time he was in this hotel, the elevator seemed to move faster today. He was still determining his approach when the elevator ding alerting him to his arrival on floor seven. He immediately stepped off, took a quick survey of the floor, and found what he was looking for on his right down at the end. He started in that direction. As he walked, he stuffed his hand into his pocket, activated the device and kept with a non-aggressive approach.

"Excuse me," he said in his best disarming voice. "Is it possible I can get a few extra towels? I was looking for the housekeeper on our floor but didn't see her." He trailed the sentence with a smile.

As he spoke, he hoped his proximity was close enough for what he needed. He'd done his research on the best skimming devices to magnetic data from cards without the need to swipe the card. Many of the hotels had gone to the system that allowed guests to either utilize their cellphone as the key to enter their room or a hotel key tapped against the sensor attached to the door. Like the credit card industry that utilized contactless payments, the cards used by the hotel had a flaw.

The RFID chip inside the card was constantly emitting a signal. Many astute holders of said cards use faraday wallets that prevented the signal from being hijacked by the new and improved skimming devices. But while that worked for your everyday consumer, it would be a hassle for the cleaning crew of a hotel.

So as he smiled at the woman reaching to grab him some new towels, the data from her master keycard was being downloaded onto his device.

"Thank you so much," he said when she handed him the towels. "You have been a big help." He took the stairs down one flight and entered the corridor for the sixth floor. He strode with purpose toward his destination. As he stood outside of room 613, the moment of truth lay before him. He retrieved the device from his pocket and placed it next to the reader. After three seconds, the light turned green and the magnetic lock disengaged.

Troy smiled as relief flushed his body. And unlike the episodes in the car, his hand greedily reached for the handle, turned it, and entered the room belonging to Detective Elise Porter.

15

"So where do we go from here?" Porter asked as the line for coffee inched forward.

"Now we go find our killer."

"Excuse me, but I could have sworn that's what we were doing over the last few days."

"Well, now we have an additional piece of information that we didn't have at our fingertips before. We know our killer has some flesh removed from his body. I'm willing to bet it's something that can't be easily concealed. Probably near the neck or face."

"And what makes you so sure of this?"

"Our killer has been meticulous, so he likely took precautions to ensure he wouldn't leave DNA. My guess is he was fully covered. Brandy has already told us the victim was not sexually assaulted, so there would not be a reason for him to be undressed."

The line moved forward, and Porter shot Sampson a dubious glance.

Sampson continued, "The only portion of his body that was likely exposed was the neck and face area. From what we know about the killer, I'd bet he wanted the victim to see his face and to fear him."

"Great! That narrows it down to all the men in the world who have nicked themselves shaving."

"Next," the barista called, summoning Porter and Sampson to the counter.

"I'll take a black coffee, large."

"OMG! Detective Sampson, is that you?" the girl with the pink hair asked. "The last time you were in here, it was with Special Agent Donatella. I could never forget such a hand-some, rugged, attractive face."

Sampson searched his memory bank. He recalled coming to Brent's Coffee shop on Trade Street with the special agent, but he was having a hard time placing the woman who stood before him. At the time he was preoccupied with a sadistic killer who'd taken out the entire board for Global Insights Security. It was his first case as a detective, one that afforded him the opportunity to work side-by-side with the lovely Donatella. Although he wouldn't admit it, there was a connection he felt toward her. One that he wished he'd acted on, but given the high stakes of the case the timing wasn't right.

The barista frowned at the lack of recognition. "Well, my name is Margaret, and one day she and I will be partners. I've helped her out on a couple of cases already, and I look forward to us taking down bad guys together. Anyway, a friend of Donatella's is a friend of mine. Consider your order on the house."

They completed their orders and watched as their drinks were expertly and effortlessly made. They each thanked the young lady and dropped a few bills in the tip jar as a thank you.

Porter picked up where their conversation had left off, "So how do you suppose we find our suspect with just a scratch."

"I don't know just yet, but I'm working on it. In the meantime, let's enjoy our drinks and conversation. Speaking of which, how is the hotel living?"

"Hopefully coming to an end," she said with a broad smile on her face. "I spoke with my realtor, and if nothing goes wrong I'll be in contract on a place by the end of the day. It's a seller's market and the last thing I want is a bidding war. I'm already near the top of my budget, but I really don't want to lose this place."

"It'll be yours, and it's something worth celebrating if you ask me," Sampson said, raising his cup and tapping his to hers. "And once you're settled be sure to throw a housewarming party. John Pix gives the best gifts, and Taylor Lutz makes the best apple pie."

"Not so fast. I can't afford to get ahead of myself. First, I need to secure the place. Next, I need to see if my bank will allow me to secure an emergency mortgage. It can take 48-hours or less to process and the fee can be a little higher, but It'll be worth it to be in my own place again. Then and only then we can talk about your idea."

Sampson refused to relent, "Well, I'm confident it's as good as yours. I'll start phoning the department so they can clear their calendars."

Porter threw her hands up in mock surrender and he continued, "So now that we have a few minutes, and I'm sure you can't wiggle your way out of it, why don't you tell me a little more about yourself."

He watched as she shifted in her chair and sat her coffee on the table separating them. Her eyes lost focus and exhibited a far-off glare. He could almost envision the gears churning in her head as she carefully curated her next words.

"There really isn't much to tell," she offered. "I have

siblings, my dad passed away years ago, and I pretty much like to keep my private life private."

"Okay, well how about something different? We all have dreams of what we will be when we grow up. Mine was to be a professional football player. But for a multitude of reason, that didn't work out. I even thought about being a chef. I must admit that I'm pretty good around a kitchen. But circumstances in my life drove me to being a detective. And to be honest, I don't miss out on either of those other dreams. Nonetheless, they are a part of my past, at least my past dreams. So how about you? What did you want to be when you were younger?"

Her eyes cleared and she was back in the present. "I had my heart set on being a model."

Sampson interrupted, "I could see that. I bet you would have been great at it. Why didn't you follow through on your dreams?"

"Let's just say there were a multitude of reason that didn't work out." She cracked a smile, and he did the same. "After that I wasn't sure what I would do until becoming a cop made sense. Once the thought crept into my mind, it was the only thing I thought about and, as they say, the rest is history."

"Well, the modeling industry's loss is the Charlotte PD's gain. I'm glad you're on our team." He drained the remains of his coffee and said, "Now, let's go find us a killer with a scratch on his face."

16

Troy still felt the high and exhilaration from earlier in the day. The voices in his head congratulated him on a flawless execution and urged him on the next step in their plan. They all agreed the episode at the hotel would be the hardest to pull off, but this next part would require the most skill.

Upon discovering Detective Porter's younger brother, Edward, was locked away in a mental institution, Troy began pondering the best way to make contact with him. He didn't know if his visit with him would yield anything useful, but he lived with the motto that nothing ventured was nothing gained. Therefore, he would take the drive and extract from him all useful information.

But there was still the matter of obtaining the rights to visit with him. The plan he devised was a Hail Mary at best, but he was committed to this course of action. Prior to making the two-hour trip to Triangle Springs, Troy conducted research on the facility. They had semi-private rooms equipped with full bathrooms. A fitness center for their guest to utilize as part of their stay. They had group therapy sessions in addition to private sessions. But the most important part, they had visitation open every day of the week.

He pulled into the parking lot and maneuvered away from the entrance. He needed time to observe the flow of the place before he made his move. The flow of traffic in and out of the building was in line with what he expected. But he still hadn't seen what he was waiting on to make his move. He looked at the clock, *I have time.* And while he had plenty of it at his disposal, he didn't have to wait much longer.

He watched as medical professionals walked into the building and kept a keen eye on their attire. *Simple enough,* he thought as he opened the driver's side door, popped the trunk, and looked through his options. *This should work nicely.* He shrugged into his white lab coat and proceeded in the direction of the door.

He walked into the building and cheerfully spoke to the receptionist working the front desk. He didn't wait for the response and continued down the left side of the hall. He shifted his eyes left to right and then right to left. He wanted to understand the lay of the land as best he could on his first pass of the establishment. At the end of the hall, he climbed the stairs to the second floor and made a single pass on that floor. He made his way back down to the ground level, satisfied with what he saw, and continued with his plan.

Upon his entry into the building, he took note of the name tag on the receptionist. He returned to the front desk, "Hello, Jane, I need to spend time with Edward Porter today. Where is he currently?"

She looked up at him and gave him a wide smile. "Let me check on that for you, Dr. Rush," she said, stealing a glimpse of his name tag. He's in his room for the next two hours."

"Thank you, Jane, and what room is that?"

She gave him a quizzical look and he could tell she was on

the fence. He flashed her a smile, which she brushed off but still provided the information. "He's in room 221."

"Thank you, I'll head right up to see him."

Troy left the receptionist desk in search of room 221 with a curl on his lips.

It didn't take long for him to locate the room once he was on the second floor. He gave it a gentle but firm knock and said, "Edward, it's Dr. Rush. I'm coming in, if that's okay with you." He didn't receive a response in the affirmative, but he also hadn't been told to go pound sand. He tugged at the door handle and opened it just enough for him to slide in.

At this time of the day, the room received a generous portion of natural light. The curtains were fully drawn, and the entire room was bathed in sunlight. At the table in the corner of the room, a gaunt male sat scribbling away on a tablet. His hair was blonde, like his sister's, but it was cropped close to the scalp. He was dressed in black athletic shorts and a plain white t-shirt. His bare feet were tucked underneath him as he hunched over the table, laser focused on his work.

Troy saddled up next to him, "Whatcha got there, Edward?" he asked watching as he manically scribbled away."

"Portrait," was the single word reply.

Troy looked down, and with all the squiggly lines on the paper a portrait was the last thing he would have guessed.

"It looks good, Edward. But why don't we give it a rest for a few minutes so you and I can chat? It's been a while since our last conversation, and I wanted to pick up where we left off," he lied. "In our session, we spent some time talking about your home life. In particular we covered ground on your two sisters whom you love very much."

He watched as the pressure of the strokes darkened the lines on the page.

"How about we start this session by talking about your older sister, Elise?"

At the mention of her name, he stopped drawing and for the first time looked at Troy. The intensity firing from his eyes bore into Troy's soul. The feeling he had in that moment was one he never felt before and one he couldn't explain.

"Why are you asking about my sister?" he asked locking eyes with his visitor.

"It's an important part of therapy to determine the relationship our patients have with their family members. It helps us and you when you talk about them so you don't lose touch with the real world."

The way that Edward watched him gave Troy the sense that he was seeing right through his lies and deceit. A few tense minutes elapsed before Edward said, "I miss Elise. I still remember when it was just the two of us before my baby sister, Emma, was born. She was my best friend, and I was hers. We spent all our time together after school and during the summer. But when Emma came, Elise had to split her time between me and her. For so long it had only been the two of us, but with our baby sister it wasn't the same."

He went back to his picture, but he kept talking. "I had become comfortable with our arrangement and sharing my sister, and then things changed again. Elise told our mom something that she hadn't confided in me. She told my mom she wanted to become a model. Surely, I thought my mom would turn her down, but instead she encouraged it. If my sister became a model, I would lose her forever."

He pressed harder on the paper, and the lines grew darker, "I remember the night before she was to go and meet her agent. She was filled with nervous energy. She fell asleep before I did, and I remember the prayer I made before I fell asleep. I prayed to the Lord not to let her become a model.

The following day after the meeting, she came home so upset that she marched straight upstairs and into her room. I followed in her wake and tentatively knocked on the door. She simply said, 'Come in Eddy.' When I walked in, her nose was red and puffy and her eyes were swollen. She then said, 'She didn't like me, Eddy. She said I wasn't pretty enough to be a model.' She burst into tears yet again. In that moment, I was conflicted with emotions. I hated to see my sister so devastated, but I was happy I would not be losing her."

Edward went back to drawing his picture, and for Troy that was perfectly fine. He'd already gotten what he came for. There was no need for him to stick around any longer. He said his goodbye and headed out the door.

When he left, Edward made two more strokes of his pen against the paper. He flipped the drawing upside-down and there staring back at him was the man who'd just left his room.

17

D etective Porter entered room 613 ten minutes after 8:00 pm. The curtains in her room had been drawn open and the Charlotte skyline was on full display. The tempered glass windows held the sounds of the city at bay, and the mint left on the pillowcase was a welcome gesture. She flipped the light switch on and did the same with the lamps anchoring both nightstands. Her modest nature meant she typically closed the curtains before undressing. But, she was six stories up, and so with no buildings in her direct sightline tonight she threw caution to the wind. Furthermore, the call she'd been expecting from her realtor finally came through.

Tomorrow morning, she would go to close on the house that she wanted. Her fears of a bidding war were negated when the seller asked how soon the buyer was willing to close. Porter advised her realtor she could close the next day if afforded the opportunity. This played like music to the seller's ears as they were moving to Japan and didn't have time to deal with a long closing process.

She was with Sampson when she received the news. Her

involuntary scream startled him into nearly crossing the center lane into oncoming traffic. "I guess that's good news," he'd said at the time, correcting the vehicle in his lane. He seemed happy for her and already started talks back up about the housewarming. She was over the moon with the news, but there was something nagging at her.

She couldn't help but feel like the case was spinning around but going nowhere. She appreciated the find by the ME, but that wasn't enough. She needed something that would link this killer to Hugo. Sampson didn't agree with her, but her gut kept telling her he was involved. Proving it was a totally different matter.

She walked into the bathroom, started the shower, and walked back out. There she set her gun on the nightstand, unbuttoned her blouse, letting it fall to the floor, and stepped out of her pants. A hot shower allowed her time to think, and tonight she would need a long one.

She walked back into the bathroom to test the water, *just right,* she thought, shaking the water from her hands. She pulled back the curtains and stepped in. While the water pressure wasn't what she'd become accustom to at her house in Asheville, she could tolerate it for one more night, maybe two. *No more than three,* she mused as she began to lather her hair. With her head under the water, she thought she heard a sound. The sound of a door opening. She dismissed it as sounds of the water playing havoc on her hearing. Or it could be thin walls allowing in sounds from her neighbors.

She rinsed the soap from her hair, squirted conditioner into her palm and began to massage it into her scalp. As she did, she started running through the case again. By all accounts, the most recent victim had been taken shortly after the discovery of the first. The killer was spot on with details that had not been given to the press. And she was sure Hugo was at the center of it all. But then a scary thought popped into her head.

What if someone in the department leaked the unknown facts to the killer. She tried to wrap her brain around this thought, but the more she tried to process it, the less it made sense. What motive would a cop have for helping out the killer, unless it was a fellow officer who committed these murders. She thought for a moment and then felt a cold draft creep into the shower. Or it could simply have been that the water was losing heat.

She proceeded with her shower routine while simultaneously trying to dismiss the thought of a colleague doing something so horrible. Whoever it was, they were sick, and she couldn't imagine someone in the department who was that far gone. But then again, what did she know? She was new to the area, to the department, and she didn't know much of anything about the people she worked with. Similarly, they didn't know much about her.

She took a divergent path in her thoughts, realizing that her partner, Sampson, was only trying to get to know her. But she had been cold and dismissive. She didn't relish the thought of discussing her past, but she also realized if the two of them would form the trust they needed as partners she would need to open up.

Again, she felt the cool draft invade the warmth of her shower. "Is anyone there?" she asked feeling foolish. Logically she knew no one was in there with her, but she had to ask. And if she did receive an answer, what would she do? Naked and covered in soap, she wouldn't be able to mount a great defense, but it would make it impossible for an assailant to obtain a firm grasp on her.

As she expected, no voice returned her call. But now with her train of thought wrecked it was time to wrap up this shower. She rinsed the soap from her body and the conditioner from her hair. Once complete, she stepped from the shower, grabbed her towel and began to dry off. She quickly ran it through her hair, opened her eyes, and that was when she realized something was off.

ON THE WAY back from Triangle Springs mental facility, Troy thought up an ingenious idea without the aid of his voices. In fact, he knew it would make a great chapter in the book he was writing. This thought meant he would need to make a slight detour on his way home, but he knew it would be well worth it.

The appearance of Detective Porter took longer than he expected, and he already had to let Beth know he would be late. Her voice hinted at her tiredness from dealing with the baby all day, but he had to do this. He'd find a way to make it up to her, but the day and now the night was all about the hunt.

When the detective arrived, he waited a few minutes before going in, because he already knew where she was headed. Furthermore, the micro camera he placed on the picture would provide him the details needed. After three minutes elapsed, he exited his vehicle and casually walked into the hotel. *Act like you belong here and no one will question it,* he thought to himself.

By the time he entered the lobby, the app on his phone chimed alerting him to movement in the room. He opened it up as the lights illuminated the dwellings. He watched as she left the frame, presumably to go into the bathroom. His suspicions were confirmed when he heard the shower running.

When she reappeared, she began undressing and started up to the sixth floor.

By the time he reached her floor, Porter had already returned to the bathroom. He pulled the device from his pocket and walked down the hall. *Act like you belong here,* he thought. He placed the device against the reader, and this time it immediately turned green.

He could feel the adrenaline pulsating through his veins. He could hear the relentless sound of his rapid heartbeat pounding in his ears. As he turned the handle and stepped into the room, he felt truly alive. He didn't know how long he had, but the proximity, the audacity, the danger were a rush. It all made him feel something unlike anything he'd felt before.

He held down the handle as he gently closed the door so the latch didn't make a sound. He walked into the room, where he noticed her service weapons sitting on the night-stand. How careless, he thought as he picked it up. It was heavier than he imagined it would be and not a weapon of skill. *Just point and shoot, how hard can it be,* he thought. He prepared to set it back on the nightstand and then changed his mind.

He made his way to the bathroom door. On the other side he could hear the shower running. He opened the door and stepped in. The smell of her body wash was intoxicating. He was so close to her that if he took two steps forward, he could easily reach into the shower and touch her. But that wasn't the plan for the evening. Tonight was just a dry run. A dry run in which he would leave a few surprises.

He was quick to finish up in the bathroom, and as he walked back into the main room he heard her call out, "Is anyone there?" He nearly answered out of habit and chided himself for it. That could have been disastrous. He finished up what he'd entered her room to do and stepped back into the hallway. As he did, he heard the water stop and thought, *Have fun, Detective.*

WHEN PORTER OPENED HER EYES, she looked over into the mirror as she prepared to brush her teeth. When she did, she saw the words, "Hi there!" written in the condensation on the mirror. She pondered this briefly, trying to make sense of what she was seeing. She recalled from movies that you could write on a mirror, and it would only become visible when steam hit it. So her mind rationalized this was a prank by the cleaning crew. But the nagging voice in the back of her mind told her this was incorrect. When the hairs on the back of her neck began to prickle, she moved into action.

She dried her feet to gain traction and wrapped the towel around her body. If someone was there, she'd be ready for a fight when she walked out the bathroom. Prepared to act, she yanked the door open and stepped out. A quick visual survey of the room revealed no one was there. At least no one was standing. She turned in the direction of the door and confirmed it was closed and locked.

A thought ran through her mind that the perp could be crouched beside the bed, hidden out of sight. Without taking her eyes off the far side of the room, she began to strafe in the direction of her nightstand to retrieve her gun. She reached down searching for the grip, *nothing*. Her eyes darted in the direction of her outstretched arm. Her gun wasn't there, but her peripherals caught site of it. She turned back to the head of the bed and there it sat, on the pillow next to the mint.

At this point, she started to wonder if she was going crazy. She could never recall a time in which she left her gun sitting on her pillow, yet there it sat. She picked it up and proceeded across the room. She could tell from her vantage point that no one was in between the room's twin beds, which meant the only remaining spot was the space between the second bed and the window.

She cautiously proceeded, arms locked, hand next to the trigger. She took her final two steps and to her surprise and relief found nothing and no one. She breathed a sigh of relief and dropped her arms to her side. That was when she noticed an extra set of towels, folded neatly at the foot of the second bed. She searched her memory, trying to recall if they were there when she went into the shower. She could have sworn they weren't, but she could have sworn her gun was on the nightstand too. And that clearly was not the case.

Your mind's getting the best of you, she thought as she collapsed on the bed. She needed to give her heart some time to regulate prior to completing her routine and calling it a night.

18

I t was a humid morning on this overcast Charlotte day. Sampson was deciding between driving with the windows down to get some fresh air or blasting the air conditioner and staying cool. He opted for the best of both worlds with the windows halfway down and the air set to sixty-eight degrees. Some would consider this a waste of good cool air, but Sampson looked at the problem differently. With the rush of air pushing through the windows, the cool air hit him faster and provided immediate gratification.

He was sure if his new partner was cruising along with him, it would have been one or the other, likely the air conditioner. But today she was off finalizing the deal for her new home, and for the first time since she arrived in Charlotte he was back to rolling solo. Upon her confirmation of PTO, he decided today was as good a day as any to seek the guidance of his old mentor, Bruce McMillian.

Bruce had been the instructor for the incoming cadets, and from day one Sampson felt he held a grudge against him. During PT, Bruce singled him out for dogging it as they ran, although Sampson had been fifth out of the twenty-two present. At the shooting range, he would critique his stance and his bullet placement. The abuse, as Sampson saw it, boiled over the day Sampson arrived fifteen minutes late to class.

HE HAD BEEN on his way in when he happened upon a two-car head-on collision. The driver traveling southbound looked to be at fault as he was facing the wrong direction three quarters of the way into the northbound lane. The driver, an eighteen-year-old boy, managed to pull himself out of the wreckage and into safety. But the driver of the van, a thirty-four-year-old mother of two, had been knocked unconscious from the deployment of the air bags.

Sampson raced into action only to realize the mother had her two children strapped into their car seats, and the smell of gas became ever present. He reached for the handle, and to his dismay the doors were still locked. With the mother unconscious and the kids strapped in their seats, he ran back to his vehicle, grabbed his retractable baton and smashed the passengers side window. Next he reached for the lock, cutting himself on a shard of glass he neglected to clear once the window was broken, and unlocked the door.

With the doors unlocked, he yanked at the sliding rear door and impatiently waited on it to glide open. When he had enough room to maneuver, he unlatched the child in the seat closest to him and shimmied into the vehicle to unlatch the second child. All the while speaking as calmly and urgently as he could to rouse the sleeping woman.

With the second child free from the restraints, he picked up the little girl, slid back to the exit and pulled up the little boy as well. With both kids in tow he ran back to his vehicle, opened the rear door and dropped them off inside.

With the amount of gas that he smelled, he feared his time was running short, but he didn't hesitate. He ran back to the van, opened the driver's side door, and called out to the woman again. She was still unresponsive, and the clock was ticking. He reached across her body and pressed on the seatbelt latch only to find it was jammed in place. He pulled the foldable hunting knife he carried from time to time, thankful he had it on his person today. With one deft motion, he severed the seatbelt, crouched toward the woman's midsection, and tossed her torso over his shoulder. He backed from the car as quickly and carefully as possible to ensure he didn't bump her head against the frame of the vehicle.

Once they were both clear, he stood to his full height and lumbered in the direction of his car. And not a moment too soon. Not knowing how much time they had left and not wanting to risk anything, Sampson continued to the other side of his vehicle away from that of the wreckage. The van exploded in an array of yellow, orange, and red with metal flying in all directions. He involuntarily ducked as shrapnel flew harmlessly overhead. In the distance he could hear emergency crews speeding to their aid, in his estimation not a moment too soon.

WHEN HE WALKED into the door, Bruce decided to make an example out of him. He had him recite a saying that was told to the class on a regular basis. "Early is on time. On time is late. And late is unacceptable." He then asked the young cadet, "So what does that make you, Mr. Sampson?"

In answering the question, he could feel his fury building. On this day, the day in which he saved three lives, Sampson grew tired the reprimands and questioned the treatment in front of the entire class. Bruce ignored the question, advised

Sampson to take his seat, and he went on with the day's lesson.

When it was time for the day's session to end, the class was dismissed, and Bruce asked Sampson to stay behind. He closed the door with the departure of the final student, walked to where the students had been seated and sat in the chair across from Sampson.

"Carl, why do you think I'm so hard on you?"

The immediate thought that ran through Sampson's mind was, *because you're a self-righteous prick.* But instead, he said, "Beats the hell out of me."

"Well then," he said, loosening his tie. "Let me inform you. When I look at this class I see a lot of cadets who will go on to have a good future in the police department. But I only see one who has the opportunity to have a great future. That student is you. Right now you are settling for being one of the best instead of showing you are the best. There is no one as naturally gifted as you are, but when you are not fully applying yourself, you are leveling the playing field for everyone. I want you to be true to yourself and true to your gifts. I want you to give it your all versus giving just enough. I want you to pull the class with you to match your strengths instead of you minimizing yourself to match theirs. I want you to lead."

Bruce stood from his seat, "But in the end it doesn't matter what I want. I can only push you. But it's you who has to want it for yourself. Then and only then will you be the best version of yourself." He began walking toward the door, opening it and turning around. "By the way, great job on saving the mother and her two children. I hear they are going to make a full recovery."

. . .

SAMPSON PARKED his vehicle outside the modest two-story home of Bruce McMillian, unsure of his intent. One thing for sure, it would be nice to catch up with the man who helped to steer him in the right direction when he started at the academy. He exited the vehicle greeted by the stifling heat without the aid of the air conditioner. He bounded the four steps, crossed the porch, and rang the doorbell. He could hear assertive footsteps growing closer from the other side of the door.

It swung open, "Carl," the gruff voice said stepping aside to clear the entrance. "I can't say that I'm surprised to see you here. Come on in."

Sampson entered and headed directly to the living room. After graduating from the academy, Sampson and Bruce grew close. After the stern lecture, Sampson pulled it together, and his talents shone through. When Sampson pondered taking the detective's exam, it was right here in this room that he and Bruce weighed the pros and cons. In the end, Bruce said, "Let's face it, you didn't come here to seek my advice. You came to seek my blessings. Carl, you were born to be a phenomenal detective. You just need to get out of your own way."

And he had been right. Sampson had been looking for the green light from the man who seemed to know him better than anyone else. And in a way, the nod of approval was the last step before he would jump in with both feet. But today was different. Today he truly needed the older man's counsel more than he'd ever needed it in the past.

"Let me guess. This has to do with the discovery of the girl who'd been located with similar injuries to that of the victim in your previous case."

"Yeah, it does," Sampson said, wondering how much he would be willing to share.

Bruce situated himself in his La-Z-Boy while eyeing the

detective, "But I sense that's not what is bothering you. It has to do with the fact you have already put a man away for this type of murder, and another one out of the blue is like a punch in the stomach."

Sampson knew this was the moment of truth. He'd driven all the way out here to speak with Bruce and if he wasn't going to be completely honest, then what was the point. He said, "Well, not exactly."

The older gentleman sat forward in his chair and said, "Why don't you tell me everything?" So, he did.

He told him that shortly after they arrested Hugo, he received his first call from the man admitting to the murder and informing him that they had the wrong man. He went on to tell him how the killer taunted him and stayed one step ahead the entire time, while he and he alone was frantically searching for the latest victim. While he didn't have an opportunity to do anything about the first victim, he had been given clues to save the second victim. And it was that failure haunting him today. But at the same time, he didn't have room to lament, because the killer informed him that he already had another victim in mind and that he would give Sampson every opportunity to save her. He finally admitted he had not brought this to the attention of his partner or his superior.

Bruce listened to the story, digesting every word and careful not to interrupt. When Sampson confirmed the story was done, the older man sat back and rubbed his chin while he thought. The silence was becoming unbearable until Bruce finally spoke.

"Well, son, you've certainly gotten yourself into a pickle. You should be able to talk to your partner and your boss about this."

"I wish I could, but they are both fixated on the wrong things. Porter is determined the connection is with Hugo. So much so that she has blinders on to the possibility of it being anyone else. Captain Marshall is playing the political game. For him, he would never admit we incarcerated the wrong man, because it would hurt his ambitions. I knew if I couldn't gain the backing of either one of them, there is no reason anyone else would believe what I have to say."

"Carl, I know it seems like an uphill battle, but if you go at this alone, someone is bound to get hurt. Your best option is to come clean with Porter and the both of you tackle this case together. Otherwise, whoever the killer has in their crosshairs will be the next victim."

Sampson knew Bruce was right, as he always was, but he wasn't sure he could tell Porter just yet. The two finished up their discussion, and Sampson saw himself out. When he fired up the car and prepared to leave, his phone began to ring. He picked it up, "Hello!"

"Hello, Detective. Looks like you are once again failing at your job, because I'm sitting here staring at the woman you are supposed to be protecting."

19

P orter sat in the Charlotte stop-and-go traffic thinking back to the previous night. The whole evening just seemed a little off. She wasn't one to believe in ghosts, but how else could she explain the weird occurrences in her room?

She shook her head to rattle the thought from her brain. Because today she would be closing on her house, and she could move out of the crazy hotel room. But first she had to make it to the realtor's office in one piece. This was one of those rare moments she wished she had an old blue light to attach to her hood and blow through traffic. But alas she was just like every other civilian sitting on the highway waiting to arrive at their destination.

She never understood how people were stuck in traffic jams in the first place. If everyone kept moving at the posted speed limit, traffic should continue to flow. Yet every day in cities across the country people sat in traffic. *Maybe it's the civil engineers' fault,* she thought as the car in front of her inched forward just enough to allow her to jump on the exit ramp.

Her in-car navigation read that her destination was the

first right off the exit. She looked at the time on the dashboard and realized she would be late, but only by a few minutes. Furthermore, what would they do? The deal couldn't be cemented until she signed on the line, and only at that time would they be paid for services rendered. She pulled into the parking lot, found an open visitors spot right next to the door, maneuvered into place, and placed the car in park. She checked her hair and makeup in the mirror, and after confirming everything was still in place she hopped out of the car. She rushed toward the door, not because she was late but because the heat was already in the mid-eighties, and it would only get hotter as the day went on.

Her heels tapped rhythmically on the tile floor as she crossed the lobby. "Hold the elevator please," she called out to the man who had just stepped onto it. He did as requested, giving her a moment to squeeze in with him.

"Thank you," she said angling for the corner. "Do you mind hitting floor five?"

"Not at all," he said in a professorial voice. He pushed the button for five and followed it up with the button for six. "What brings you in today?" he asked, flashing her a smile.

"Closing on my new home. I just moved into the area, and luckily I was able to find a place so soon."

"Congratulations! It took me and my wife way too long to find a home. But it was worth the wait. We love where we live now." The elevator dinged on the fifth floor, "Looks like this is your stop. Good luck and congratulations again."

"Thank you," she said stepping past him and out the door. In that moment she realized that he had a fresh cut on his face. She smiled and thought to herself, *just one of the millions of men who cut themselves shaving.* She heard the elevator doors shut behind her as she made a straight line to the receptionist.

TROY CONTINUED to ride the elevator to the sixth floor. When the doors opened, he stepped off, nodded to the receptionist, and proceeded in the direction of the stairwell. There he descended the flight of stairs until he reached the ground level. The main lobby had been empty when he entered, so he decided to exit in the same manner in which he arrived.

Back at his car, he relished at how fortunate he had been. While laying in bed unable to sleep after visiting Detective Porter's hotel room, he decided he needed to know more about her routine. He woke up an hour earlier than normal, prepared for his day, and then drove directly to her hotel.

He'd been camped out in the parking lot for fifteen minutes before she made an appearance. He anticipated she would head straight to work, but he wanted to see if she had a special coffee spot she regularly visited prior to starting her day. Instead, he was surprised when she began driving in the opposite direction of the station. This was something he hadn't suspected.

He followed as she expertly weaved her way through traffic and became annoyed when he found himself stuck in the morning traffic jam two cars behind his prey. It was hard enough to tail someone with the normal flow of traffic, but it became increasingly worse in standstill traffic. They could opt for a hasty decision and force their way into different lanes or exits for which he'd be powerless to react without being compromised.

He also had the option to pull directly behind her vehicle, but that too brought risk. When stuck in traffic, drivers spent a lot of time checking their rearview mirrors. He didn't want the detective spending that much time looking at him. So, he stayed the course and hoped any decision she made he could react fast enough to keep pace. And luckily enough for him, his gamble worked.

When she made the decision to exit the highway, he had a clear path to do the same. It meant he would spend two car lengths in the berm, but without the presence of law enforcement nearby it was a safe enough gamble.

He followed as she entered the parking lot for a commercial building. There was no signage on the building denoting the occupant, so Troy surmised it was shared by several companies. He parked three spaces over from where she stopped. He hurried from his vehicle, watched as she tended to her hair in the mirror and entered the building.

From inside he could see her approach. At five paces from the door, he called for the elevator, which had already been sitting on the ground floor. He stepped on and as he expected, she called out for him to hold the elevator, for which he was more than happy to accommodate.

Now as he sat in his car, he realized how fortunate he had been. With the detective preparing to move into a new home and out of the hotel, he needed to solidify his plans and accelerate his timetable. He had some time to kill, so he picked up his burner phone and dialed a familiar number.

When the call was answered he said, "Hello, Detective. Looks like you are once again failing at your job, because I'm sitting here staring at the woman you are supposed to be protecting. I gave you the first clue, 'Objects in this mirror are closer than they appear,' but it appears you have squandered it. Detective, at this rate you'll be searching for a victim that you should have saved."

"Why don't you tell me where you're at? I'll meet you there and we can settle this mano a mano."

"In due time, Detective. In due time. For now, I recommend you pay closer attention, because the next time you hear from me it will not be a social call."

Troy settled into his seat and patiently awaited Porter's return.

20

"Earth to Sampson," Porter said while taking another bite of her bacon cheeseburger with extra pickles, hold the onions. "I lost you there for a moment. What's on your mind?"

Sampson had been weighing the pros and cons of telling Porter the truth as his mentor Bruce suggested, but he was still reluctant to do so. The more he attempted to pinpoint his reasoning, the more elusive it became. He rationalized more time was needed so he could lay all his cards on the table, beginning with the call the night they arrested Hugo. Yet with the passage of time, coming clean now just didn't feel right. At least not at this moment while they enjoyed lunch.

"I was just wondering how closing went today. You have officially established roots, so you are a Charlotte resident."

She grinned ear-to-ear, "It all went so well. Aside from signing papers until my hand went numb, the only delay was transferring the downpayment. I had the wrong routing number. But once that was squared away, the remainder of the process was seamless."

She pulled two keys from her pocket and dangled them in the air, "And then these puppies became mine."

"You do plan on changing the locks, right?"

"Of course, it's the first thing I'm doing when I get home tonight. Receiving the keys from the realtor is a symbolic gesture. I already had the new smart lock sitting in the car awaiting its new home."

"I can be handy at times, and it just so happens my evening is completely free," he said plastering a grin on his face. "Not to mention I have a set of tools in the trunk of my car, and I know a slew of killer take-out restaurants around town."

"Detective Sampson, you drive a hard bargain. I'd be honored and willingly accept your assistance."

"Good, now that's settled, I had a thought about the case. For the sake of argument, let's say all this time Hugo has been telling the truth, that he didn't kill Mandy. That means the killer had to have access to his house in order for the trophies from Mandy to end up there. I think we need to have another discussion with Mrs. Wolfe. We need to know if there was anyone else who could have easily gone in and out of the house."

"But what about the truck that was found with Mandy's DNA? How do you explain that and the fact the truck is registered to Hugo?"

"Logically, you explain it the same way. If someone had access to his house, they could have easily swiped his driver's license."

"Right...the mysterious person who broke into a house stole a driver's license and planted evidence. Do you know how absurd that sounds?"

"Yes, which is exactly why the person is getting away with

it. You've said it yourself, it's so hard to believe that it just could be true."

Porter polished off her fries and washed it down with a sip from her Coke. "Say you're right. What would have been the motive to frame Hugo?"

"Opportunity, maybe. Unless the killer had a grudge against him or a score to settle."

Porter wiped her mouth with her napkin and said, "We asked both Hugo and his wife this question already, and both couldn't imagine any such person."

"Do you know everyone who has it out for you?" Sampson asked, raising an eyebrow.

"I'd like to think I do, but I see your point. The mysterious person could have something against Hugo that Hugo himself wasn't even aware of."

"Exactly! And if that was the case, that person could easily have slid under the radar, completely undetected." He watched as she began to rearrange the facts and suppositions in her mind.

"Okay, so what's next?"

"We talk to the wife. We find out who they may have been close to and who else had access to their home. We then do some investigative work to see if any of them had a secret hatred of Hugo. With any luck, we'll be able to narrow down our suspect pool and nab our killer."

"Sounds rational enough. Mind if we tackle it tomorrow? I would love to get the locks to my new home changed."

"Works for me. Let's check out and then make our way there."

IN THE RUNNING car across the parking lot at Bad Daddy's burger joint sat Troy Evans. When Detective Porter finished the purchase of her new home, he was prepared to make his way to campus. Instead, the voices in his head urged him to follow her, to see where she would go. The internal battle raged on as the external host followed cautiously behind.

They had already crossed paths earlier that day. The last thing he needed was to be spotted in her rearview mirror while she drove. Any good detective always prided themselves on their personal security. And doing so in a car was second nature.

As a result, he was three cars away doing his best to keep an eye on her every move. If he sensed the light would turn red and he'd be caught on the wrong end of it, he switched lanes, sped up, and then maneuvered his way back into position once he cleared the intersection.

After twenty-minutes of him trailing his prey, she pulled into Chesterfield Commons. It was one of the new sub-divisions in Waxhaw, an up-and-coming suburb of Charlotte. All of the lots in phase one were sold, and they were beginning the grading process for phase two. Troy recalled Bethany wanting to look at a house in this area, but it was much further away from the university than he wanted, so they nixed the idea.

Now as he looked upon the houses and the size of the lots, he could see why his wife had recommended a viewing. Nonetheless, he was happy with where they lived, and for the moment the only thing he needed to be concerned with was the address for Detective Elise Porter.

He watched as the detectives carried on with their conversation. He watched as Porter smiled, played with her hair, and smiled some more. He watched as she scarfed down her food and took liberal drinks of her soda. *To be a fly on the wall,* he thought as he drank from his insulated coffee cup.

He hoped that the detective was enjoying this meal,

because her moment was drawing ever so close. And with the purchase of her new house, he was now altering his plan on the fly. It was imperative he made his move before she moved out of the hotel, or all the nights he stayed up planning would have gone to waste, and he would need to start over. And he didn't want to, because the plan he constructed was ingenious. So much so, he had already written the chapter in his book about and he dreaded the thought of having to write a new scene to match a new plan. Therefore, the best option was to accelerate the timeline.

Once the detectives completed their meals, they made their way to the counter to pay, and he headed for the parking lot exit. He said out loud and to himself, "I'll be seeing you again real soon, Detective Porter. And then you'll meet your monster."

21

Sampson and Porter arrived separately at her new home located at 2821 Turtle Drive. The curb appeal was the first thing to grab Sampson. The walkway was lined with decorative walking lights. The flower bed was filled with an array of flowers that he could not name if his life depended on it. All he knew was they were gorgeous, and they highlighted the entrance to the home.

The hedges had been expertly trimmed and all uniform in appearance. Sampson loved a green lawn, and he had to admit this one outdid his, but only slightly. The edging was crisp, and the blades of grass were soft.

The exterior of the home wasn't a letdown either. It was filled with windows, which meant it would receive plenty of natural light. Not to mention the red brick that made up the remainder of the house.

They exited their cars and stood at the walkway. "This house is amazing," Sampson said on his approach.

"I know, right? I had to have it. It was right at the top of my budget, but I decided it was go big or go home. And now I'm the proud owner of easily the best home on the block." She said this last bit with a smile. "Come on, let me give you the grand tour." Sampson hefted his tools and off they went.

By the end of the tour, he had to admit the inside was as amazing as the outside. Whoever designed this home had done a phenomenal job. He made a note to himself that he would need to find out who it was and have them design his next home.

They made their way back to the entrance, where Sampson got to work uninstalling the existing locks.

"Alright, Porter. You've dodged me long enough. As payment for my services today, which normally I would do free of charge, you have to tell me something about yourself I don't know. Which shouldn't be hard because you have been keeping your life a secret. But it can't be something like I scraped my knee playing a game of pickup ball as a youth."

"Well darn, that really did happen. Guess I can't use that now," she said with a smile.

He returned the smile. "Ha ha. Seriously, tell me something good. Something worthy of this added protection I'm adding to your new abode."

"You sure are an insistent booger, aren't you?"

"Yep, I am. Now spill."

She thought for a few minutes and then offered, "Okay, so we talked about our dreams as kids about what we want to be when we grow up. If I recall correctly, your dream was to play football."

"Correct. Some memory," he said with a smile.

"Anyway, I told you when I was young I wanted to be a model. Well, here is the rest of the story."

Sampson raised an eyebrow.

"As I look back on it, there wasn't any particular reason. I just thought it would be something cool to do, and I thought I could be good at it. To this day I can still remember telling my mom about it and she said, 'Elise, honey, I have faith you can be whatever you want to be.' That was enough for me. I went full speed ahead. I practiced my walk, my posture, my stances. I just knew I would be great at it."

Sampson could sense the "but" coming and waited for the other shoe to drop.

"I researched agents and found one that I thought would be a great fit for me. I managed to secure an appointment with her, and I was on top of the world. My mom, who at times could be void of emotion, seemed genuinely happy for me. Without having to ask, she volunteered to take me to the appointment.

"The morning of the meeting, I was a nervous wreck. I was preparing to launch into a career at a young age. It was intimidating and exhilarating at the same time. When we arrived, the agent saw us immediately. Since I was underage, my mom was allowed to sit in on the meeting with me."

Porter shifted her weight uncomfortably. "The agent, Mrs. Banks, asked the perfunctory questions. Why do you want to do this? Do you understand the commitment? Etc. I answered each one in turn and felt everything was going well. She then said, 'I like your gumption, kid. You have spunk. But there is one problem. I'm not sure you're pretty enough to make a successful model. You may get a job here and there, but nothing to springboard your career.'"

Sampson stopped turning the screw and looked over at his partner, speechless and unsure what to say. She pressed forward.

"My mom and I thanked her for her time, and I couldn't wait to leave her office. My dad had always taught me to be tough, so I refused to give her the satisfaction of seeing me cry. But the moment we stepped out of her door and was out of view, I collapsed into my mom's waiting arms and cried my eyes out. She tried to make me feel better by saying, 'What does she know? There are plenty of other agents out there. We will just go to one of them.' But the reality was, it was too late. That one phrase crushed my dream of ever being a model, and I gave up on it before we were settled in the car for our return trip home."

Sampson found his voice, "I have no clue what she had been looking at. You're a knockout."

Porter smiled, "Thanks, but you don't have to do that. It's a dream I let die a long time ago."

"I'm not doing anything. In fact, there's been something I've been meaning to ask you. In two weeks, our department will be hosting the annual party. It's an opportunity for those of us in uniform to let our hair down and to have some fun. As it turns out, I've yet to ask anyone. Would you mind being my plus one to the captain's ball? Hands down you'll be the prettiest girl there."

Porter smiled ear-to-ear. "I'd be honored."

22

Troy Evans nervously paced the walking path between the bed and the television in room 611 at the Home2Suites hotel. Hours of preparation. Days of watching. Sleepless nights of due diligence. All of which led him to this moment. He sensed the adrenaline spiking and the voices in his head were ominously quiet. For what else could they say? It was all up to him now. He was the one who would need to carry out the mission and finish the story.

For the fifth time tonight, he heard footsteps bypass his room. The previous four were all false alarms, other patrons headed to their temporary accommodations. It amazed him how many people were on this side of the floor. It added an element of risk, but nothing he couldn't handle if the need occurred.

Earlier in the week, he called the hotel and requested room 611 specifically. He gave them the excuse that it was there that he proposed to his wife eleven years ago this week. He laid out the story that things were not as spontaneous and romantic as they had once been. So, he wanted to recreate the scene and ask her again for her hand in marriage. Expecting her to say yes, they would renew their vows and start again with a fresh slate.

Marcy, the young lady he spoke with, said it was an excellent idea and the room would be ready for their arrival. The hotel expected them tomorrow, so that meant no one would be staying in the room on this evening. As such, that provided him with all the time he needed to enact his plan.

He continued to listen as the footsteps slowed. It wasn't until he heard the lock disengaging next door that he realized he was holding his breath. He took one last look around his room to ensure everything was in place and he waited. Her routine dictated she would head to the bathroom, turn on the shower, and then come back to the room to undress.

He waited. The sound of the shower was his next key. It also signified the most important moment of the evening. He counted backwards, 5, 4, 3, 2, 1.

He gently pulled open the door to the adjourning room. In order for this to happen, it required that the room be unlocked within each room. As part of his preparation for the evening, he let himself into room 613, unlocked the door, and exited as quickly as he entered. Back in his room, he unlocked the door as well and swung it on it hinges. At the time it made an audible creaking sound that just wouldn't do. He retrieved the can of WD-40 from his back, lubricated each hinge and repeated the process until the sound abated.

Now as he opened the door, the only sound that could be heard was that of the shower pounding against the tile. He continued to inch it open, not wanting the movement of the door to alert her of his presence. More of the room came into focus with each movement of the door. And then there she was.

Porter had her back to the door and was unbuttoning her shirt, unaware that he had just entered her space. Troy was careful to ensure each move was purposeful and each breath was silent. She slid the top from her shoulders and tossed it on the bed. As she did, Troy took the tentative step into the room. He felt he should be moving faster, but he couldn't justify the risk. He knew he had time as long as he kept moving and didn't second guess himself.

Porter began undoing her trousers, and as Troy inched closer he could smell her perfume mixed with her body chemistry. In that moment it reminded him of Mandy. Her smell was that sweet, seductive, sinister.

She unbuttoned her pants and immediately unzipped the zipper. When the pants fell to the floor, Troy sprang into action.

With her pants around her ankles, her mobility would be compromised. He planned on taking her by surprise, but he wanted every advantage he could get.

His swift motion informed her that she was not alone. But it was already too late. Before she could turn around to face her would be attacker, Troy wrapped his left arm around her neck and with his right hand placed the chloroform-soaked rag across her nose and mouth. The speed in which he moved and her compromised state gave him the upper hand in this situation.

She reached back, trying to grab hold of his hair or to gouge out his eyes, but the drug was beginning to have its effect. Her frantic arm motions slowed, and her body fell limp. He held the rag to her face for an additional five count to ensure she was truly out. Satisfied she couldn't cause any trouble, he lay her on the bed, walked into the bathroom, and turned off the shower.

He returned to the room, picked up her pants, and spread them across the bed. He placed her limp body in a fireman's carry and crossed the threshold to his room. There he dumped her on the bed and sized her up. *It'll do*, he thought as he looked over at his newly purchased Samsonite Silhouette 17 Spinner Garment Bag.

———————

THE CALL SAMPSON received at the end of their shift from the killer didn't make any sense. "We can't all be the prettiest girl at the ball." On his drive to his house, he played the thought over and over in his head. "We can't all be the prettiest girl at the ball." He thumbed his fingers on the steering wheel trying to decipher this latest riddle.

The courteous *beep-beep* from the car behind him pulled him from his daydream. He looked up to realize the light had turned green, and just as he prepared to wave at the driver to thank them, the billboard on the opposite side of the road caught his attention.

The billboard, a Belk advertisement, showcased a family sporting the latest wears. A succession of thoughts swirled through his head.

"When I was growing up, I wanted to be a model. I even went down the path of trying to hire an agent. But the first agent shattered my dreams when she said that I wasn't pretty enough to be a serious model."

"Would you mind being my plus one to the captain's ball? Hands down you'll be the prettiest girl there."

"We can't all be the prettiest girl at the ball."

The driver in the car behind him laid down on the horn. It was all so clear to him now. Porter was the target. He did a U-turn against the oncoming traffic, receiving another round of drivers blowing their horns.

He picked up the phone and dialed, "Come on, Porter, pick up the phone." Her voicemail immediately picked up. "Shit!"

He smashed his foot on the gas, blowing past the slowing traffic and bursting through the intersection. He hit redial and was greeted with the voicemail yet again.

"I'll charge my phone when I get to the room," she said upon realizing her phone died at the end of their shift.

'How could I have been so stupid?" he yelled slamming his palm against the steering wheel. *She's a well-trained police detective and can handle herself,* he thought as he slowed just enough to turn the corner. But a sinking feeling in his gut was warning him it might already be too late.

He parked the car in front of the hotel's entrance and raced into the building. Alarm registered on the face of the staff as they witnessed this crazed man running in.

Sampson reached into his pocket and flashed his shield, "Detective Sampson, Charlotte Metro PD. I need the room number for Elise Porter."

"I'm sorry, sir, we don't pass that out –"

"This is a life and death situation. I need you to provide me with the information now."

The employee looked flummoxed until the manager stepped in.

"I can help you over here," she called from the end of the counter.

Sampson covered the space in three strides.

"Let me see," she said banging at the keyboard. "Elise Porter, correct?"

"Yes!"

"She's in room 613, let me get you a key."

Her words fell on death ears as Sampson was already sprinting toward the elevator. The car arrived just as he prepared to press the button. In his rush to hop onto the elevator, he bumped into a patron in a blue hat and blue jacket rolling a suitcase.

He mashed the button for the 6th floor and repeatedly pressed the close door button to expedite the process. He called her phone again. *Voicemail.* "Damn it!"

The elevator dinged at the sixth floor, and the doors slid open. He raced off looking for her room. When he arrived at 613, he banged on the door.

"Porter, open up!" He banged again. "Come on, open up!"

Upon hearing the commotion, patrons from the other rooms begin cracking their doors to see what was going on.

Realizing he wasn't going to get an answer, he backed against the wall across from the door. With all of his might, he kicked at the locking mechanism. The door gave slightly but not enough. Again, he kicked at it while hearing in the background, "Oh my God. I'm calling the police."

His third kick shattered the door jamb and the deadbolt, but the safety latch still hung on strong. Breathing heavy, he kicked the door one more time, and it finally gave way.

It was clear before the door flew open that she was not inside. His only hope was she had not come straight back to the hotel. But this notion was completely dismissed when he saw her clothes laying on the bed and her weapon laying on the nightstand.

23

S ampson slouched against the wall while the technicians combed over the room. After kicking the door in and then seeing Porter's belongings, he immediately called into dispatch, officer missing. Martin and Sanchez where the closest to the hotel when the call went out, and they were on the scene in two minutes.

Kirby and Jenkins were the next to arrive, followed by Smith and Torres. Sampson gave Martin and Sanchez the make and model of her car and then dispatched them to go search for it in the parking lot. He sent Kirby and Jenkins to begin speaking with the neighbors on the floor and then Smith and Torres to go secure the surveillance videos.

Sampson impatiently awaited the crime scene tech's arrival, which came three minutes after Smith and Torres. They dawned the necessary gear and began searching the room. He was mentally replaying his actions when Captain Marshall appeared.

"Sampson, what in the hell is going on?" He barked as he lumbered down the hall.

He hadn't decided how much he would tell his boss, but he knew he had to tell him something.

"I received a phone call from the person claiming responsibility for the death of Brianna Armstrong. His cryptic message led me to believe Detective Porter was his next target. I immediately came here, obtained her room number, and found her room empty and her belongings in place."

Martin and Sanchez came rushing down the hall, "Her car is in the lot," Sanchez said. "Doesn't appear any foul play took place in or around it."

"What do you mean you received a call from a person claiming credit for the murder?"

Jenkins exited the room closest to the stairwell followed by Kirby. When they joined the other members from their department Kirby spoke, "We finished interviewing everyone on this floor. Aside from the mad man kicking at the door, they didn't notice anything unusual."

Sampson shook his head, trying to restart the replay in his memory. Something didn't add up. He replayed the moment he raced down the hall and banged on her door. The doors opening around him, revealing people trying to ascertain what was happening.

"God damn it, Sampson! What more do you know about this case that you aren't telling me? Why would the supposed killer be calling you?"

Sampson heard the voice of his captain, but the words were muted as he continued to replay the scene.

The first two kicks and the door barely budged. With the third kick, the door jamb gave and so did the deadbolt. But it required a fourth kick for him to gain access to the room. He walked past Captain Marshall and into the room. He looked at the door and a memory from his mind's eye finally caught. Not only had the deadbolt been engaged, but the security latch had been as well.

He entered the room, "Detective, you're not supposed to be in here."

He ignored the protest, walked over to the adjoining door, and that was when he noticed it. The lock on this side of the room was not locked. He pulled a pair of gloves from his pocket, slid them over his hands and reached for the doorknob, turned, and pushed. Locked.

He walked back into the hallway, pushed his way through the crowd outside and stepped over to room 611. He signaled over to the manager who had been standing in the background.

"I need you to open this door."

She eyed him, deciding between opening the door or telling him no. She turned and looked at the door for room 613 and decided opening it would be the financially sound option.

"No one is staying in this room," she said, placing the key to the card reader. "In fact, we have a nice couple planning to reenact their proposal in this room tomorrow." Sampson yanked at the door the second the lock disengaged, and his mind's eye flashed a vision of what he might see.

Porter posed on the bed. Skin removed from her body but the face still intact. A backpack with her skin neatly tucked inside. A lock of her blonde hair taken as a trophy. Another life loss because he couldn't save her.

Instead, when he burst through the room, expecting to see the worse, he saw nothing. The room was empty. No backpack, no body, no murder. He looked around trying to see if there were any clues to help him understand what happened to Porter.

"Sir," the manager called. "As you can see, there isn't anyone here. Now I must ask that we vacate as this room has been reserved for tomorrow."

Sampson rejected the pleas from the manager, because

something was off. The bed, which is typically made in a pristine fashion, looked as if it had been disturbed. The subtle smells in the room reminded him of Porter. He began to canvas the room's interior. He pulled open the drawer for the nightstand, finding nothing out of the ordinary. The surfaces were all clear. Then he spotted it.

He bent over, reached into the trashcan, and retrieved a sales tag. It appeared to be from a Samsonite roller bag. His mind replayed the scene of him running across the lobby in search of the elevator. Upon his arrival the doors slid open, and a man exited. His mind replayed the audio that he had been filtering out at the time. "Excuse me, sir," the man said, pulling the bag from the car. He slowed the scene down in his mind, *the bag seemed heavy on its wheels*.

"No!" he said as he pushed his way out the room and to the end of the hall. He snatched the door to the stairwell open and began his descent. He moved down at a reckless speed, twice running into the wall at the landing, once nearly losing his balance. He burst through the door on the first floor and ran toward the exit.

Outside, the heat and humidity of the day hit him like a brick wall. His eyes were wild, and his breath was ragged as he raced through the lot looking for the suitcase, looking for the killer. He spun around, checking to see if there was anyone there. Nothing. No one. He heard the bodies exiting the hotel and the footsteps quickly approaching.

"What is it?" Kirby asked trying to identify the risk that the rest of the department onsite hadn't noticed.

"He was here," Sampson said turning around to face the assembled group. "He exited the elevator at the time I was entering. He had Porter with him, and I didn't notice."

They looked at him with bewilderment. "How could you have not seen her with him at the time?" Smith asked.

"Because he had her tucked away in his roller bag." We need to scrub the footage for that floor and these exits. He was in a blue shirt and a blue hat. We –"

His phone vibrated in his pocket. He pulled it out and immediately answered, "Yes."

"Late as usual, and to think you were so close. But all's not lost. You have 48 hours to save her, but not a minute longer."

The call disconnected, and Sampson eyed the group. "Two days to find her, or she's dead."

Detective Elise Porter's eyelids felt as if weights were attached to them. Her mouth was completely dry, and her frontal lobe throbbed against her skull. Although she had regained consciousness, she stayed still. Something about how she was feeling didn't seem right. When she tried to recall her last memory, the pain overtook her thoughts.

She changed tactics and tuned her ears to the ambient sounds around her. She could hear the forced air cascading around whatever building she was in. She heard the subtle sound of fabric shifting. *I'm not alone*, she thought as she continued to process the room. She didn't hear any sounds from outside. *Am I in a warehouse? Not necessarily, it could be residential and nighttime.*

She shifted to her sense of smell and noticed nothing. At least nothing she could discern. *Hospital room? Have I been injured and being prepped for surgery? That doesn't make sense. If I was in a hospital room, there would be all kinds of sounds.*

She took inventory of her body making minute movements. Toes, feet, and calves were all in working order. She mimicked placing her hands on the home keys of a computer keyboard. All fingers were good as well. Her brain sent signals to her wrist, and that was when she noticed something was wrong. She could feel the rope pressed against her skin. It wasn't tight, but it was tight enough to keep her wrist tethered to something unseen.

She reached back into her memory. She needed to remember what happened She fought through the pain and the fog. Glimpses of her in her hotel room. Shower running in the background, her blouse already laying on the bed. She was unbuttoning her pants. A nearly imperceptible sound followed by rapid movement.

It all came flooding back to her. Someone was in her hotel room, grabbing her around the neck. A sweet smell tantalizing her nose. The abduction, the ropes. She'd been kidnapped. Then realization hit. She'd been kidnapped by the killer they'd been hunting.

Panic was slowly beginning to creep in, but she needed to stay calm. For the moment, she was alive, and that was important. She opened her eyes, slowly. She looked around, orienting herself to the surroundings. The neutral paint on the walls signified she was in a residential building, not commercial. She could sense the window nearby, but no daylight entered the room, *certainly nighttime*, she thought. She pulled at the restraints on her wrist. Not much give and tighter than she originally thought. Although she hadn't noticed it before, she soon realized her ankles were restrained too. She suddenly became self-conscious when she realized that she was still in her panties and bra.

The overhead light flickered on, "Well hello, Detective Porter."

She searched the room the invisible voice, "Who's there?"

"Let's not play coy, Detective. I'm sure you have a really good idea of who I am. Or at least, what I am."

She held firm and didn't respond.

"What's the matter? The cat's got your tongue? You had plenty to say to the news reporter the other day. Let me see. What was it you said? Oh yes, 'What we know without a shadow of a doubt is that the individual we are dealing with is deranged. Anyone who preys on the innocent is evil. But to do what he is doing to these young women is deplorable. We will overturn ever rock until this person is locked away.' You see, Detective Porter, it's not nice to cast dispersions. Especially when you don't know who could be lurking around the corner."

As he spoke, his voice grew closer.

"While you've been looking for me, I've been watching you. Your drives back and forth to work. Several times while you and Detective Sampson enjoyed a meal. And don't let me get started on him. He's the reason, at least part of the reason, you find yourself in this predicament. But I digress."

She could feel his body heat a mere two to three feet from where she lay restrained.

"But alas, the stars have aligned, and you and I have been afforded a few days to hang together."

He came into view and a memory came flooding back, "I know you. You were the guy on the elevator at my realtor's office."

"Bingo! And also once in the elevator at your hotel. You really should pay more attention, Detective."

She thought back and recalled he was on the elevator. He exited on her floor and walked to the end of the hall. *How could I have been so careless?*

"What do you want with me?" she managed to ask.

"What do I want with you?" he repeated. "That is a loaded

question. It's not a matter of what I want with you. It's what I want for this world and of Detective Sampson."

He pulled over a rolling chair that was near the end of the bed. "This world is going to hell. These promiscuous women who think the world should cater to their whims. They need to realize there are consequences for their actions. And since the world is too blind to it or is unwilling to do anything about it, I needed to step in."

As he spoke, Porter began to believe Sampson had been right. Could this be the person behind it all along?

"I'll tell you like I told your partner after the first murder. Mandy deserved what she got, and so did Hugo. Did you know she slept with him so he would change her grades? And not only that, he made her agree to sleep with him longer in order for the grade to be changed. It was sick. He had to be stopped. She needed to be stopped. And girls like her need to be stopped."

His eyes turned cold and dark. "I refuse to have my daughter live in a world like this when I can do something about it."

"And what exactly does this have to do with me?" she asked.

"You're a blonde."

She stared at him, and he stared back at her as if that statement cleared everything up.

"And then there's the matter of your partner. I gave him every chance to prevent this from happening. I provided him with clues that tied directly to you. If he figured out you were next on the list before," he paused for a second, "this. Then you wouldn't be here. It unbelievable how little he knows about you and your life. So, he failed to save you, just like he failed Brianna."

Sampson had a chance to save Brianna, she thought. "What are you talking about?"

A sardonic smile creased his lips. "Let me guess. He hasn't shared any of our communications with you. Why exactly are you partners if you don't know anything about one another and you don't share crucial details with each other? I gave him every chance to rescue her before she met her fate. I gave him clue after clue. And he failed to piece the evidence together in time to rescue her. So, this time, I gave him the opportunity to prevent the abduction from happening in the first place. And again he failed. Makes me wonder why he's a detective in the first place."

Porter couldn't believe what she was hearing. Had Sampson been given the information to save Brianna? Had he been given the opportunity to prevent her from being abducted? Her head was spinning, and the headache was coming back.

"But even with his latest failure, I've given him more time to find you, but he will not receive any additional clues other than those I have left for him. We shall see if he can earn the title of detective. Because his failure will mean your life."

"My God, Sampson! You mean to tell me the killer had been in contact with you all this time and you told no one?"

"Captain, I told you on several occasions that I didn't believe we had the right man in prison for the murder of Mandy Cox."

"Yes, Detective. But what you failed to mention is you had been in contact with the killer."

"Let's face it, Captain, had I told you what would you have done?" He waited a beat and continued. "You would have done nothing, because you continue to let your career political ambitions get in the way of doing what is right."

With each passing sentence, the voices raised to another level. So much so the other detectives on the floor could hear every word.

"Watch yourself, Detective. You are already on extremely thin ice!"

"And yet you can't deny it, because you know it's the truth. If I believed for a minute bringing this information to you would have been received with the desire to find the truth, I would have done so. But instead I found myself having to chase down this monster alone."

"And that's exactly where you are going to find yourself, alone! You have been nothing but trouble since you found your way into my department. It's clear you are not a fit."

"Well, that's something we can agree on. You aren't fit to lead this department."

The color in Marshall's face drained, and then he barked out, "That's something you don't need to worry about, because as of this moment you are suspended pending investigations of your actions or make that lack thereof."

"Suspended? I think not. I'm going to find my partner."

"No. You. Are. Not. You have done enough damage. We will find Detective Porter. You can turn in your shield and your gun and vacate the premises." Marshall held out his hand waiting for the aforementioned items to be dropped into it.

Sampson unclipped his holster, reached his hand into his pocket to retrieve his badge, and then placed both on the captain's desk. He stood from his seat, opened the door, exited, and slammed it on his way out, shattering the glass. He heard Marshall's voice, but he was already tuning out the words. He may have been suspended, but he had no plans of quitting this investigation. He would locate Porter without Marshall's blessing or assistance.

THE DRIVE to his home passed in a blur. His mind raced on what he needed to do. He looked down at his watch. It was now 11:00 p.m., three hours into the 48-hour deadline. Although the hour was late, he knew where he would start. But before he did. He needed to go home and acquire a few things.

He unlocked the door, walked in, and disarmed the security system. He proceeded to his coat closet, where he kept his gun safe tucked away at the top of the closet. He pulled it down, entered in the six-digit code, and retrieved his Heckler and Koch VP9. He took the time to load the clip before shoving it into place. Two minutes after entering the house, he was back in the car and headed to his destination.

So far, the killer had been getting the best of him. At every turn he was numerous steps ahead, and in order to save Porter Sampson couldn't afford to be playing from behind much longer. The hour at this time of night allowed him to drive faster than he had earlier in the day. He'd conduct this interview and then see what thread it allowed him to pull next.

Twenty minutes later, he found himself at the home belonging to Mr. and Mrs. Hugo Wolfe. As he figured, all the lights in the home were extinguished, but this was a life-or-death situation. He didn't have time to wait until morning.

He stepped from the vehicle, temperature still in the mid-eighties, and proceeded to the door and rang the doorbell. It took a second ring of the bell before he heard movement in the home.

The light in the foyer came to life, and Mrs. Wolfe looked through the window next to the door. She immediately recognized Sampson and began to unlatch the door.

When the door swung open, she had a dour look on her face. Sampson realized the hour of the night and him appearing unannounced could be misconstrued that some tragedy may have happened to her husband.

"Yes," she said in a tremulous voice. "Is it..."

"No," Detective Sampson interrupted. "Nothing happened to Hugo."

She had a visible sigh of relieve. Despite everything she'd heard about his infidelities and the fact he had been convicted of his lover's murder, she still cared for him. "Do you mind if I come in for a few minutes?"

It was clear she was confused by the visit, but she stepped aside and ushered him in. He took the familiar route to the family room and took a seat on the couch. Mrs. Wolfe sat across from him in the chair.

"Mrs. Wolfe, I'm going to level with you. I believe your husband may be innocent of the murder of Mandy Cox."

The defensive posture she'd taken once seated gave way to confusion.

"I have reason to believe someone else committed that murder and that same person is responsible for the murder of Brianna Armstrong that has been in the news this week. At first the department believed this was the work of a copycat, but I'm not sold on that idea."

A stream of tears lined both of her cheeks. She grabbed a tissue from the box next to her and wiped her face.

"This killer has abducted another person, my partner, and I only have two days to find her."

"What is it you think I can do to help you?"

"Before Detective Porter was taken this evening, we planned to come visit you tomorrow. We were working off the premise of your husband's innocence. If that was the case, we needed to review the case with fresh eyes. Evidence that was used to convict your husband had been found here in your home. If your husband was innocent, as we now believe, that means someone had access to your house to plant that damning evidence. Can you think of anyone who could have come and gone? Someone who may have had a key?"

She thought for a minute and then said, "At the time of the murder, we had an electronic key lock. So we never had the need of giving someone a key only a keycode. Hugo could always generate one on the fly if needed. And to my knowledge, we just had the one that allowed us to come and go. About a month after his conviction, I couldn't remember the code or how to operate that darn thing. So, I had a locksmith come out, remove it, and replace it with an old-fashioned deadbolt lock."

A thought emerged that Sampson hadn't considered. If the killer had access to Porter's room, how did he get it without having an actual key? The hotel burned a copy of the surveillance video, but before Sampson had a chance to review it, Marshall demanded a meeting in his office. During the meeting Sampson laid everything out for him, thus leading to the suspension. But he didn't have time to think about that.

Electronic keys can be hacked, and he was certain this was how the killer gained access into Porter's room and the room next to hers. He needed to see the video. He'd have to figure that out later, for now he pressed forward.

"We asked this before, but could there be anyone who held a secret grudge against your husband? Someone who wasn't outwardly hostile to him, but maybe despised him because of his second job as an erotic author?"

"No, no one. Hugo was beloved by everyone he met."

"Well, it's clear if he did not do it, someone went through a lot of effort to frame him for Mandy's murder." He decided to change tactics.

"Had there been anyone in your home around the time of the murder?"

Sampson could see the gears moving in her head as she tried to recall a memory. "We had a party with friends to cele-brate the release of Hugo's fourth novel. That's the only time we had guest in our home for a few months."

"Do you have a list of the partygoers?"

"Hugo handled the guest list, but I think he had a copy in

his office." She stood from the chair, a renewed pep in her step with each stride.

Sampson didn't know what would come of the list, but he gained two pieces of information he didn't have before. The killer likely used a device to hack the lock to Hugo's house, and if Mrs. Wolfe could locate the invitees to the party, he'd have a fresh group to look into.

Her efforts to locate the list didn't take long at all. She came back with two pages of names and handed them to the detective. "Here you go. With the fact there is someone else who committed this horrific crime, does that mean my Hugo will be let free?"

He knew better than promising anything, so he simply said, "That'll be a matter for the courts. But if we can apprehend the person who is truly responsible, it'll go a long way to expediting things." He knew she would likely have more questions, but in the back of his mind he knew the clock was ticking on Porter's life.

He stood and said, "Thank you for your assistance this evening, Mrs. Wolfe. I appreciate your willingness to help. I'll see myself out." He walked in the direction of the door and thought, *Time to pay a visit to the precinct.*

26

As the clock struck 2:00 a.m. in the city, the exterior of the Charlotte Metro Police Department was calm and silent, like the rest of the city. But behind the doors, detectives, patrol personnel, sergeants, and the captain were in a coordinated flurry.

One of their own was being held hostage, and they now had 42 hours before a mad man who showed no compunction about killing in the most gruesome way planned to do the same to her. Captain Bradley Marshall was front and center leading the effort.

The surveillance video from the hotel for the day of the abduction didn't yield much. They watched as the suspect entered room 611 lugging the roller bag Sampson had noted. According to the manager on duty, a master key utilized by the housekeeping crew had been used to enter the room. But all keys had been accounted for when they took inventory.

At approximately 6:30 p.m. Porter entered her hotel room. The hallways stayed empty until 7:15 p.m when the male exited room 611. The next sighting was that of Sampson running down the hall in search of Porter's room.

The suspect in the video managed to hide his features from the view of the camera throughout the hotel. Worse, they lost track of him leaving the hotel because he hadn't parked in the lot. He simply strolled out of the view of the outside camera, rolling his bag.

Marshall assigned Kirby and Jenkins to canvas the area around the hotel for additional cameras. If they were lucky, they'd be able to locate him from an adjacent company's video feed. In the meantime, the video had been given to the forensics team to see if they were able to glean anything that couldn't be picked up by the naked eye.

The CSI group that processed the room noted there were many fingerprints around the room. Nonetheless, they ran them through AFIS, the Automated Fingerprint Identification System, and returned a total of ten males. They were looking for anyone with a criminal past who they could then go and speak with. So far out of the ten, three were persons of interest. Marshall dispatched three teams to pay each man a visit. Detective Smith questioned the need to awake them at this early hour to which Marshall made abundantly clear they would wake up the entire city if they had to.

By the time 3:00 a.m. hit, Marshall had his entire unit focused on locating Porter. He scoured the map of the city asking himself, *Where are you?* He took another drink of his coffee that had been reheated twice and was growing ever stale.

"Somebody brew a fresh pot of coffee! This is going to be a long day!"

MEANWHILE, two floors down from where Marshall was commanding his squad, the forensics team was hard at work processing the surveillance video frame by frame. They tried to catch images of the suspect when he passed some glass, a mirror, or any surface that reflected images. Early in the process, they thought they hit pay dirt with an image on the elevator, but the only thing the captured was his chin. They notated the abrasion on its edge.

Sandra, the team leader, received the call shortly after midnight to rush into the office. Dispatch apologized for waking her, but in reality she was just heading to bed. She was scheduled to be off the next two days and had been out celebrating her sister's engagement. She had one, maybe two drinks more than she should have for someone who was on duty. She'd already had two cups of coffee and headed to the break room in search of her third.

As she strolled down the hall focusing on not dropping her ceramic cup, she was unceremoniously pulled into the conference room that lined the hall.

"What the hell!" she exclaimed as a firm hand covered her mouth.

"Sandy, it's me, Sampson," he said shushing her into silence. "Please, keep your voice down."

"Sampson, you damn near scared me to death," she said, clutching at her chest and nearly dropping her mug. She eyed him, best she could through her haze, "Did I hear correctly through the department gossip that you were placed on suspension?"

"Yes, but that doesn't mean I'm giving up on finding my partner. That's where you come in."

"I don't know. From what I heard, Marshall was very clear that he did not want you working the case."

Sampson sighed, "Sandy, I'm aware of the captain's orders. But I will not sit back and wait for my partner to be murdered by this psychopath. So again, I'm asking for your help."

Sandy sensed the sincerity and determination in his voice. "I never liked the arrogant SOB anyway. What do you need?"

"What have you found from the videos so far?"

"Honestly, not much. We've been looking at everything between noon and the moment you arrived on the scene."

"Is that all the hotel supplied?"

"No, they provided the last seven days, but Captain Marshall's direction was to scour that segment frame by frame. I have Bobby and Phil focused on that as we speak."

"Can you give me a copy of the full seven days?"

Her initial expression had her leaning toward saying no and finding a reason to justify her answer. But instead, she said, "You're going to owe me one."

"You know I'll pay you back in full."

"How about this, you go fill my mug with coffee and three sugars, while I go retrieve a copy of the footage. Meet me back in this room and we'll exchange."

"Thank you," he said taking the mug from her hands. I'll be right back with the coffee.

She smiled and said, "Don't think getting this coffee makes us even. You still owe me."

PORTER'S internal clock told her it had to be between 4:00 a.m. and 5:00 a.m. If that was correct, she had been missing about ten hours. If the killer was to be believed, at minimum Sampson knew she was missing and hopefully the entire department. She didn't know what they knew, but she had faith they could figure it out and rescue her. For now, she had to stay levelheaded and determine what she could do to better her situation.

Her kidnapper left shortly after their conversation and

hadn't yet returned. The entire time, she worked to free herself from her bonds, but the more she tried the tighter they became. Realizing this was a losing battle, she surveyed her surroundings searching for anything she could use to her advantage. Looking around the room, it appeared to have a fresh coat of paint and void of everything except the bed she lay on and the rolling chair.

In the academy, they taught her the proper way to subdue a suspect, but they didn't teach the best way to get herself out of a precarious predicament. She bounced her head on the bed three times, wishing she had some ingenious plan to extricate herself. After having fought the restraints all night, this last outburst sapped her of her reserves, and she immediately fell asleep.

THE NEXT TIME Porter opened her eyes, her senses were on high alert, and she immediately recognized someone was in the room with her.

"How'd you sleep?" the voice asked from the foot of her bed.

Speaking with more strength and conviction than she felt she said, "What's your end game here? You're going to be caught, and you're going to spend the rest of your life in jail."

"That's where you are wrong. I will not be caught. In fact, I could walk into police headquarters and no one would be the wiser. I'm a nobody who blends into the background. Furthermore, given the incompetence in your department, I truly have nothing to fear."

"In my line of work, those who believe they have nothing to fear get caught the soonest."

"Are you willing to stake your life on it?" he asked darkness clouding his eyes. He didn't wait for a reply. He stood and walked out of view.

The sound of a wooden drawer opening filled the room. This was followed by the sound of metal trays clanging against a solid surface. She couldn't determine his actions but could tell each one was done precise and with purpose. He was silent as he worked behind her, which made her wonder if this was the end. If it was, she would fight like hell until she was free or he had killed her.

Whatever he was doing seemed to be taking forever. When he returned the trays to the wooden drawer and closed it, she could feel the fight or flight emotion building within her. She counted each step as his foot made contact with the floor. Nine, the final tally, before he was standing at the head of her bed.

"Did you know the barbiturates used in doctor-assisted suicide can be synthesized to take longer to act? Thus, prolonging the patient's suffering. It can be considered barbaric and absolutely unnecessary. Unless, you have a good reason for prolonging the inevitable. I researched it until I found the perfect measurements to last exactly one hour. Once those calculations were solidified as accurate, adjusting the time frame was a trivial matter."

He came into view with a syringe in hand. "I advised your partner he had 48 hours to save you. That was twelve hours ago." He removed the top, squeezed out any air bubble and looked down at the detective.

"Since you're so sure they'll save you, let's put your money where your mouth is. Let's just see how good Detective Sampson is." As he drew nearer, Porter began to buck against her restraints.

"There, there, Detective. As I'm sure you're already aware, you cannot escape the bindings." He grabbed her head with a strong hand and wrenched it to the side, exposing her neck. He jabbed the needle in and pressed the plunger.

Now we patiently wait to see if your knight in shining armor comes rushing through that door prior to the deadline.

"You're a monster," she yelled to his departing form.

"The monster has yet to come out and play," he said, shutting the door behind him.

27

Sampson drank the last drop of coffee from his mug, his fourth cup in the last three hours. He'd been operating on adrenaline since Porter's abduction and turned to coffee to push him further. He could feel his energy beginning to wane, but he refused to quit. He would continue to watch the surveillance footage until he found another clue. The problem? He didn't know what he was looking for.

His eyes were losing focus, but then he saw the man fitting the stature of his suspect approach a maid cart. He checked the floor, *seven, not Porter's floor.* He prepared to disregard it, but there was something about the man that caused Sampson to watch further.

He never got close enough to the maid to take anything from her. But she did hand him a stack of towels. He graciously accepted them and once again Sampson prepared to move on. *His stance, something about his stance wasn't right.* "He's avoiding the camera," he shouted.

He watched as the man took the towels and headed for the stairs. Sampson located the view of the stairwell and watched as the suspect left floor seven and reappeared on floor six.

The suspect walked down the hall, pulled a key from his pocket and placed it against the lock. He then opened the door and walked into his room. Sampson rewound the video and looked again.

This time he zoomed in on the door lock. He noticed the man didn't have a key, but instead an electrical device. Maybe it was his phone. Many hotels moved to allowing a phone to act as a key. But this device looked nothing like a phone.

It finally occurred to Sampson that in his sleepy haze he missed a crucial piece of information. The room he used that key on wasn't his room. It was room 613, Porter's room.

A new surge of adrenaline shot through his body. It was all making sense to him. The killer didn't have a key. In fact, he used the interaction with the housecleaner to copy the master key. His mind raced and his body was already in motion.

He walked over to his back counter, where he had his phone charging, opened up his contacts, and found the number he was searching for. He dialed the number and tapped his foot while the phone rang. After four rings it was answered.

"I need to meet you, now... No, it can't wait until noon... Remember you owe me, damn it... yes, the usual spot."

Sampson disconnected the call. He grabbed his keys, wallet, dropped his phone in his pocket and snatched the paper from the printer.

"WHERE ARE WE, people? I need answers!" Marshall boomed.

"We didn't find anything useful in the videos," Sandra stated from the corner of the room. "The video feeds from the other establishments didn't yield anything useful."

Sanchez spoke up next, "We located the store where the

roller bag was purchased. We have them pulling video footage and also looking for the transaction. With any luck, he purchased the bag with his credit card and we can go nail this sick puppy."

"How long?" Marshall pressed.

"An hour, maybe two."

"We don't have two hours. See to it we have an answer in one!"

"Yes, sir."

"What are we hearing from patrol?"

"No trace of them," Dean Warner said. "It would help if we had a lead to follow, but for now we're shooting in the dark. A car, a partial license plate, an area where they were last seen beside the hotel. Once we have a nugget, we'll be on it like a dog with a bone."

"Damn it, this is one of our own. She's been missing thirteen hours and we aren't any closer to finding her than when she first disappeared."

Chad Baker, a fifteen-year department vet, said, "I have an idea that's not technically moral but may bring him to us." All eyes turned to him, curious about this idea.

"Well, tell us what it is."

"What if we spill to the media that we are investigating a killing similar to that of Brianna Armstrong? We tell them it was the same MO as the last killing. When they report it and our suspect hears the news, he's bound to want to check it out. He wouldn't want a copycat stealing his thunder. We have cameras and plain clothes in the crowd. We find someone fitting the description and we nab him. Again, not morally legal, but could help us along."

The collective group turned back to their captain to gage his reaction.

Before he could answer, Officer Blake spoke up. "I'm not so

sure that's a good idea. What if that sets him off and he kills Porter? Or God forbid there is already another body out there. Maybe he thinks we found his next victim and doesn't fall for our trap."

Baker countered. "He doesn't strike me as the guy who goes too far off script. But it's clear he craves the limelight. Look how he's killed and posed his victims. He seeks the attention in a passive-aggressive manner."

"He's clearly sick in the head, which means we don't know how he'll react. A move like this will endanger her life, in my opinion."

"Enough," Marshall said, bringing the attention back on him. He seemed to be weighing the argument and finally said, "Our backs are against the wall. Set it up, discreetly."

"I know just who to call," Baker said, picking up his phone and walking toward the exit.

As THE SUN settled into the sky and the temperature passed 90 degrees, Sampson sat in his car outside of the old Coca-Cola bottling plant. From his days of working patrol prior to becoming a detective, he liked to meet with his confidential informants off the beaten path. He cultivated his relationship with each of them so there was mutual respect. They wouldn't yank his chain, and he'd help them out of a jam, as long at the offense wasn't too grievous.

The CI he was meeting with today didn't fall into the category of his typical CI. This one had been brought up on charges of attempted murder, and had it not been for the testimony of Sampson a twenty-year sentence was waiting on the other end of a guilty verdict.

He impatiently tapped the steering wheel, feeling each

minute slip away. He found all of his informants showed up on time, except this one, but it wasn't anything new. A silver Acura MDX appeared in his rearview mirror headed in his direction, *about time*. When the car pulled up next to his, both drivers exited their vehicles.

Vivian Chase, a five-foot eight-inch brunette with silky-smooth unblemished skin, golden-green eyes, posture of a supermodel, personality of a comedian, and temper of a 40's gangster walked over toward Sampson with fire in her eyes.

"Seriously, this couldn't wait a couple hours? I had plans for brunch at Znooze, the trendy new spot that can take hours to get a seat. I'll have you know I only had two reservations in front of me before it was my turn. I'd already been waiting over an hour."

He reached back into his car, retrieved the bag from Duck Donuts. "Here, knock yourself out."

"Great, sugar and carbs. Just what I was looking for in a meal this morning."

"I don't have much time, so I'll get right to it. I need to know who can locally make a card skimmer like this?" He handed her an enhanced, blown up picture from the video footage.

Prior to beating the attempted murder charge, Vivian worked in a technology think tank. They saw all kinds of inventions during the design and implementation phases. She also kept her ear to the ground on what the black market had for sale.

She took the picture and scrutinized it from multiple angles. "What makes you think I'd have any idea about this?"

"Vivian, I don't have time for games. Tell me what you know." They locked eyes, his of desperation, hers of admiration.

"The guy you're looking for is called Chocolate Chip. I

think the name comes from him being black and he's able to process all types of information without forgetting one detail. He has several hideouts across the city and rarely is in the same place for more than two days. But every day, twice a day, he rides by his momma's house. If the curtain on the second floor is closed, everything is okay. But if it's open, it means there is danger. Let's just say, you don't want to know what happens if the curtain is opened."

For as long as he'd known Vivian, she never lied to him. So as wild as this story sounded, he knew she was telling the truth.

Just like he knew she was telling him the truth about her husband beating her and threatening to kill her and then her parents if she ever told anyone. She entrusted Sampson with the truth. He told her several times what she needed to do, but the hold her husband had on her was strong.

It was late one summer day. He came home drunk and prepared to give her punishment for being a horrible wife. Before he could start in on her, she pulled a kitchen knife from under the seat cushion and stabbed him over and over. In total there were six wounds. Her first call was to Sampson and his first call was to the best lawyer he knew and a family friend.

"Thank you," he said walking back to his car.

"You know it should have always been you," she said as he opened his door. "You were always my first love."

He slid in the car without responding but thought, *and it should have always been you too, but the timing never worked out.*

28

On the campus of UNCC, the students rushed about their business heading to classes, back to the dorm rooms, off to work, or simply to the meeting area where they tossed the Frisbee about. None of them paid attention to Professor Troy Evans as he sat on the bench under the tree partaking in his turkey and Swiss cheese on a croissant

Typically, after lecture he went to his office to grade papers or to spend some time working on his latest novel. But not today. Today he wanted to bask in his greatest conquest, which would surely translate into a phenomenal book. He had roughly three chapters remaining to write before he'd consider the first draft complete. But before he could write them, he needed to see how his real-life story would come to an end. Because after all his art was mimicking life.

He folded the second half of his sandwich in the parchment paper that had been used to secure it. He retrieved his phone from the bench and opened up his news app. Several times throughout the course of the day, he liked to catch up on the latest news. No one knew when a newsworthy event would soak up the headlines.

He figured he'd start with the local news, because then again nothing ever happened in Charlotte. The screen had to redraw while the content was pulled from the server. Once it loaded he was surprised to see breaking news dominating the headlines. The reporter from the ABC affiliate spoke into the camera.

"I'm Megan Riley with WSOC-TV reporting live from the thirty-two hundred block of Chelsea Drive. Sources from within Charlotte Metro PD have confirmed the discovery of another young girl that has been mutilated. Details are slowly coming in, but by all accounts this seems to be the work of the same killer plaguing the city. The ME has yet to arrive, but with this latest development, it's another life taken too soon. This is –"

Troy locked his phone, and his mind began racing. The voice weighed in, *this is clearly a trap.*

"You don't know that. What if there is someone out there?"

I know you're smarter than this. The reporter was vague on the details, and what are the odds that a copycat would have been found in the midst of your current engagement?

"When aren't they vague on details? If the person did what I suspect, they wouldn't want to share the details with the public."

Okay, what if it is someone else? It means nothing to us.

"It means everything to me. If there's a copycat, then we must see who's better. I think I'll stop by and see what I can discover. Furthermore, if it is a trap, we have a contingency plan already in place."

He waited for a rebuttal, but when none came he stashed his sandwich in the brown paper bag and headed off to Chelsea Drive.

"Sir," Officer Blake spoke, "we've been here over an hour with no sign of our guy. He's not going to show."

"Captain, give it more time," Baker countered. We have to give time for the perp to catch the news and then appear. We can't expect him to be here five minutes after the broadcast."

"But we can't be waiting around all day either. While we are sitting on our thumbs, Porter's time is slipping away."

"Officer Blake, you've made your point," Marshall said. "But we will need to give it another thirty minutes. If he hasn't come by then, we will wrap up this operation."

"Look alive everyone, someone fitting our suspect's description is driving up in a red Ford Bronco," came the call over the comms.

"It's showtime," Baker said, eyeing the monitor.

"Stick to the script. If this is our guy, we run a three-car tail on him. We need him to lead us to where Porter is being held. We can't afford to lose him."

For this assignment, the department released three vehicles the detectives would use. A gray Honda Civic, a blue Chevy Malibu, and a black Toyota Prius. These vehicles were ones they seized as part of the various stings executed the previous year.

Kirby and Jenkins were assigned the Honda. They would be known as car one and would start off immediately tailing the suspect. Martin and Sanchez would be operating the Malibu. Their job was to stay tucked in with the remainder of traffic. Depending on the length of the drive, car one would turn off and car two would take over.

Car three, which was being driven by Smith and Torres, would stay on the parallel street. If their suspect turned off, they would pick up trailing while the other two worked into new positions. It was a choreographed dance that if executed properly would leave the suspect never knowing he was being trailed.

"This is car one. I see him approaching."

"Car two here. We see him as well. He doesn't seem to be in any sort of rush. Should we apprehend him now?"

"No," Marshall exclaimed. "We stick to the plan. We see if he leads us to Porter's location and then we grab him. Johnson, can we run the plates?"

"Already on it, sir. South Carolina plates MGP 3289. Looks like we've got something. Ralph Leonard, age 30. Checking for known residences. He owns a home in Indian Land, just over the border."

Officer Blake spoke up, "Sir, that's out of our jurisdiction. Should we coordinate with the South Carolina Sheriff?"

Captain Marshall thought about the implications of that action. If they brought the sheriff in and he captured the suspect, the capture would go to him and his department. This would leave Marshall and the CMPD on the outside looking in. Furthermore, not capturing this madman would jeopardize his ambitions of becoming Mayor Marshall in the next election.

"No, Porter is one of ours, we will do what's necessary to bring her home."

"Sir, looks like he's leaving the vicinity," Sandra said.

"Car one is on a loose follow. If he leaves, we'll get him."

"Everyone else fall into positions," Marshall commanded.

The fact the perp was driving a red Bronco made him stick out like a sore thumb, Marshall thought. But he saw this as a sign. It was meant for him to capture this maniac, and he would do just that.

Their suspect, Ralph Leonard, left the uptown area and jumped on I-77 headed south. Car one pulled on the ramp with one car between them and the suspect. From a surveillance standpoint, they couldn't ask for better conditions. Most of the local residents were still at work, thus keeping traffic light on the freeway. But it wasn't so light that the suspect would realize he was being followed.

For the time being, the red Bronco stayed in the middle lane with a speed between 54 and 56, adhering to the 55-mph speed limit. Car two stayed in the right-hand lane roughly four car lengths behind car one. At this distance and in this location, if the suspect decided to exit the highway, car two could gracefully exit, making it look natural and not drawing any suspicion. For its part, car three was trailing behind car two and awaiting directions. If car one felt he'd been spotted, car two would rotate into the position for car one, and car three would take the position of car two.

"Be aware we're closing in on I-485, and the suspect has changed over into the right lane." Car one said. "We need to be prepared in case he exits."

"Roger that."

"Copy."

Back in the Mobile Command Center, Marshall spoke to his troops, "Don't lose track of him. I have a feeling he's leading us right to Porter. God willing, we can put an end to this ordeal tonight."

"I hate to sound like a broken record, but the route is still headed in the direction of his home in Indian Land."

Marshall shot Blake a glare. "Point taken."

The suspect did as expected, taking the ramp for I-485 and continued on that path until he exited on Johnston Road. At the exit, car one continued to drive on the freeway while car two took his place.

"I've got your six," car three said, pulling in behind car two.

As the traffic continued onto Johnston Road, the red Bronco settled into the right lane, again observing the speed limit. While the team was prepared for anything that this suspect would throw at them, he didn't make any sudden movements.

When they saw the sign, "Welcome to South Carolina," car two opened the comms, "We are still on Johnston Road, but we have just entered into Indian Land."

"Keep following," Marshall urged. "We are about ten minutes behind you in the mobile unit. If he's headed to his residence, don't make a move until I get there."

Car one spoke next, "Entered the address we found into the GPS and I'm already headed in that direction. I'll meet you boys there."

The next three minutes were quiet as everyone began running scenarios of the next steps through their minds. It was clear to the collective group if he stopped at the residence, they'd begin preparing plans to breach. They would need to do so in a manner that didn't spook the suspect into doing something rash. The last thing they wanted to do was to come this far only to have him react irrationally and kill Porter.

Car two spoke again, "We're now entering a residential neighborhood. The address we located is here, and it's a strong bet that's where he's headed. I'm going to fall back a little more. If he stops at that address, I'll continue my drive by."

"I'll set up at the end of the block," car three said.

"He's pulled in at 1975 Cougar Way. I'm breaking surveillance."

"He's exactly where we expected him to be," Marshall said. "We will stop one block over and strategize our plan of attack."

Car three, the only one with eyes on the suspect at this point, spoke, "Suspect has parked in the driveway and has entered the house. Nothing appears out of the ordinary. We're keeping watch."

Within seven minutes, the mobile command unit along with cars one and two were situated a street over from the residence of the suspect that was holding Porter hostage. The atmosphere was both tense yet resolute. They were going into this building; the questions were how and when.

"We don't have any riot gear, so we have to know going through that door he's not on the other end with a shotgun ready to blow one of our heads off," Martin said while strapping on his bulletproof vest.

"What we do have working for us is the element of surprise," Torres said over the comms from car three. "Right now, he expects we will need to use every minute he had given us to find her. He wouldn't suspect we come kicking in his door this soon."

"While that's true, he holds the ultimate element of surprise. We don't know what's behind those closed doors, but he does. You'd imagine if he went through all of this trouble, he's bound to have a surprise or two waiting for us when we go in."

"What we can't do is sit here all night and do nothing," Marshall said. "How about this. Smith and Torres, you're already there on the block. You two will breach from the back door. Clear the back and look to see if there is a basement. If it is, you hit it. You'll need to make your way to the house undetected, so proceed with caution. Kirby, Jenkins, Martin and Sanchez, you're going through the front door. Kirby and Jenkins, clear the front room, the remainder of the front room, and the garage. Martin and Sanchez, you make a straight line up the stairs. Be prepared to kick in every door if necessary." He paused, looking his men in the eyes.

"If you come across the suspect, take whatever action is necessary to subdue him, but do not kill him. If for some reason he has stored Porter at another location, we will need to find out. Are you all clear on your assignments?"

"Yes, sir," they said in unison.

"Good. Let's go bring Porter home."

In the command center, Martin, Sanchez, Kirby and Jenkins finished strapping on their vests and checking their weapons. Once they were prepared, they hopped into the Malibu that Martin and Sanchez had driven over and headed in the direction of 1975 Cougar Way.

In the meantime, Smith and Torres decided they would approach through the neighbors' yards instead of walking down the street. They had to navigate a series of 4-foot-high wrought iron fences. Luckily, they had flat tops instead of the decorative pointy tops, so finding purchase to hop them was a cinch. When they arrived at the backside of the house, they said, "Team three is in position." Less than thirty seconds later they heard, "Teams one and two are in position."

Without hesitation the call came from the command center, "Breach!"

Simultaneously the front and back doors swung inward on broken hinges. Torres was first in on the back side of the house, while Jenkins was first in on the front. Smith and Torres made quick work of the back and said, "We're headed down to the basement."

Kirby and Jenkins leapfrogged the front room, "Clear in the front, headed to the garage."

Martin led the way up the stairs with Sanchez close on his hip. Back in the command center, Marshall could feel his anxiety rising with each report out. The son of a bitch had to be in the basement or one of the rooms upstairs. Martin's voice came over the comms, "Upstairs is clear."

In a panic, both Smith and Torres spoke into their mics, "Everyone get out!"

As Troy Evans pulled into the driveway of 1975 Cougar Way, he was still skeptical that he was being followed. He'd had an uneasy feeling the minute he arrived at the so-called location of a similar victim. Upon observing the crowd, it didn't add up. He'd expected to see more of a police presence, but while there was one it wasn't like the other events. And the people in the crowd gave off a bad vibe. He counted three people who looked like cops in civilian clothing. Again, there could have been a rational reason for this, but it wasn't a scene he planned to stay for.

If they were setting a trap for him, he'd have to turn the tables on them. When he purchased the Ford Bronco, it was black. But he wanted something that the cops could easily track if it came down to it. So he had it painted red. If for some reason they were tracking him, he wanted it to be easy for them. To aid in this, he also drove the speed limit. This too meant there was no reason they'd have trouble.

The entire drive back to this house, one purchased for this specific reason, he continued to check his rearview mirror. He didn't see any cars that he recognized, but it didn't matter, because if they were following, it would all be revealed in time.

He shifted the car into park, stepped out and calmly walked into the house. Once inside, he moved with more urgency. He pulled back the edge of the carpet in the living room, removed the loose floor board and obtained his set of keys, wallet and glasses. He dropped the wallet belonging to Ralph Leonard and the keys to the Bronco into the empty space. He returned the floorboard to its spot and lay the carpet back down.

Next, he walked toward the back of the house and down

the stairs. He turned the corner at the bottom, crossed the room, and opened the door. While the door was in plain sight, anyone coming down the stairs would be preoccupied well before noticing it. He closed the door behind himself and walked the underground path that connected the house belonging to Ralph Leonard and the house of Leonard Johnson. Once on the other side, he activated the surprise he had waiting for his would-be visitors. He opened the door leading to the garage, sat behind the wheel of a grey Honda Odyssey van and opened the garage. He pulled the vehicle from the garage, closed it back, and drove off.

It wasn't necessary that he drove too far, just enough to be out of the immediate area. So he pulled into the shopping center, brought up the camera feeds on his phone, and waited. If this had been a mistake and no one was following him, he could deactivate the trap, put everything back in their proper places, and be prepared to use it again at some point in the future. But that wouldn't be the case.

Ten minutes after vacating the premises. He caught glimpses of armed policemen entering the home. "What a shame. I was hoping it wouldn't come to this. But some people never learn. Well, they'll learn today."

He watched as they worked in pairs to cover the house. *Good technique*, he thought. He watched as the three groups went their separate ways after clearing the first floor. While he had cameras upstairs, he was focused on the one down in the basement. He watched as the two officers approached the gigantic sign directly across from the steps. The one that read, "Danger, Highly Toxic." Next to it was a clock that was counting backwards. They only had five seconds. He heard them yell for everyone to get out, but it was too late.

The minute they opened the door, the toxic fumes were being jet propelled through the home's ventilation system. It was both odorless and tasteless, so they had no clue they were being poisoned until they read the sign.

When the clock hit zero, the two in the basement were the first to collapse. The two on the first floor had the greatest chance for escape, but the minute they walked into the garage they sealed their doom. There was no exit out of the garage, so as they ran back through the house, they both collapsed before reaching the door.

The two upstairs could have jumped from the window if they were aware what was happening. But the truth of the matter was they would have passed out prior to hitting the ground. Instead, they tried to run down the stairs, and both passed out before reaching the bottom. Seeing that his work for the moment was complete, he suddenly had an urge for ice cream.

I'll stop by the Dairy Queen and then go see how Porter is doing, he thought as he pulled away from his parking spot.

29

I t took greasing some palms and a pair of tickets to the Hornets game before Sampson was able to tease out the information he needed from his colleagues. Nico Williams, aka Chocolate Chip, had a blue-collar-crimes rap sheet as long as a more hardened criminal. He grew up in the city, then graduated from Duke University with a degree in computer science. Attended UNC Chapel Hill for a Masters in information science, and rumor had it he was looking to go back for his PhD.

As Sampson read the achievements of this young man, he couldn't understand why he continued to turn to a life of crime. He'd been arrested more than ten times, but they could never find the evidence needed to convict him of any crime. Nico was suspected of providing technology that kept the local drug dealers steps ahead of the police. Phones that couldn't be tapped, tracked, or cloned. Early alert systems that let them know the cops were coming, rather in uniform or street clothes.

The technical backing he provided for them kept them safe from the law. In return, if Nico had a problem, he could call up anyone in any of the gangs to have it resolved. It was common knowledge that no one in the gangs touched Nico, because he provided them all the same coverage from the law. But anytime he had a problem, he'd simply placed a call, and that would be that.

As Sampson sat in the living room of the house belonging to Doris William, Nico's mom, he wondered if this plan was a good idea after all. Doris wasn't in any peril, but in order for the bait to reel in the fish, the curtain upstairs needed to be open. Sampson had to admit it was a nice little setup. She had a remote she could press from downstairs that would pull back the curtains upstairs. It took some convincing for Doris to open the curtains. She advised Sampson she had to do it once before when a couple of guys broke into her house. Nico and six of his friends came to the house. The friends escorted the men from the house while Nico stayed to console his mother. One of the men looked over to her son and said, "We've got it from here" and then they walked out of the house carrying the unconscious bodies of the men who broke in.

Sampson promised her he wasn't there to arrest her son and didn't want any trouble. It was a matter of life or death, and he really needed to talk to him. She continued to tell him she didn't have a number for her son and couldn't be sure what would happen if she pulled back the curtains. Sampson told her to let him handle that, but it was important that he speak with Nico tonight. It took an hour, but finally she agreed to help.

The two had a cordial conversation, sipped on tea, and watched a couple episodes of Chicago PD in syndicate. Sampson checked his watch, 8:13 p.m. Porter had been missing for over 24 hours. He couldn't believe how much time he'd been at Doris Williams home and still no sign of Nico. He was beginning to wonder if Vivian had been wrong.

The vibration of his phone in his front pocket broke his train of thought. He retrieved it and read the caller ID. The call was coming from the dispatch.

"This is Sampson."

"Carl," came the rushed voice from Veronica. "There's been a tragic accident. Information is still coming in, but it appears Kirby, Jenkins, Martin, Sanchez, Smith and Torres have been rushed to the hospital. They've all been poisoned."

"What! How did this happen?"

"They were following a lead at the direction of Captain Marshall. They thought they found the location where Porter was being held. When they breached the house, that's when it happened. They've been rushed to the hospital, but Sanchez is in critical condition. It sounds like he took a rough fall down the stairs when they tried to escape."

"Shit. Okay. Thanks, Veronica. Let me know if you hear anything further." He reached to return his phone to his pocket, and before it settled back into place the front door of Doris home flew open.

Sampson was slow to react after hearing the news about the rest of his team. That hesitation had him staring down the wrong end of a double pump shot gun. Doris was quick to her feet, and Sampson was quick to speak, "Wait, I'm just here to talk with Chocolate Chip." He threw his hands to the sky and tried to give off his most non-threatening look.

In the background, he could hear Doris talking to someone saying, "I'm okay, I'm okay. He just needs to talk to you. He said it's life or death."

Sampson counted six goons. *Same number as the last time.* The girth of them obscured his vision of Nico. He tried again, "Look, Nico. I don't want to cause any trouble."

"No trouble, you say. You're in my momma's house scaring her half to death and you have the audacity to say you don't want to cause any trouble. Well, I'm sorry pal, rather you wanted it or not, you've found a whole heaping bag of trouble."

His voice bounced off the mass of humanity standing in front of Sampson until he came into view. He was short, five-five, five-six at the most. Skinny but full of sinew. His skin was a chocolate brown, and he had a bald head. Sampson couldn't help but notice the irony playing out in front of him. Nico was wearing a blue Chips Ahoy shirt and a pair of blue jeans. Had the situation not been dire, he might have started to laugh. Instead, he said, "I'm only here looking for information, and by all accounts when it comes to information in this city you are the best person to speak to. Your mom and I have been having a pleasant conversation, drinking tea, and waiting for you to arrive."

For the first time since entering the house, Nico looked at the scene that lay before him. As he looked around, the scene began to tell the story. "Guys, you can put that away. I think we are good here."

The one holding the shotgun looked perturbed. It was clear he was ready for some action, but that action would need to come another day. The six men left the house, and Nico closed the door behind them.

"Now ma, you can't be scaring me like that. This man damn near got his head blown off."

"Boy, watch your mouth. And if you kept a phone number I could reach you on I wouldn't have to go to such drastic measures to see you."

"We'll talk about that later," he said kissing her on the cheek. "Let's go out back and chat," he said to Sampson while leading the way out the door.

"So, Detective Sampson, what could be so important that you'd drag my mother into the middle of it?"

Sampson pulled the paper from his pocket, unfolded it and handed it over to Nico. "I have it on good authority that you're the person to come to when it involves a skimming device like this. Before you get on the defensive, I'm not here to bust you. I need to find the person who is using this device. He's kidnapped my partner, and I have less than 24 hours to find her before he kills her."

Nico eyed Sampson and after a few moments, looked down at the picture. Sampson could tell as he studied the picture, it was familiar to him.

"Why should I get involved in this matter?"

Sampson knew this question would come up, and now was the time he needed to settle on the answer. "I've already told you I'm not here to bust you, but understand this. This device can be linked back to you. It was used to break into my partner's hotel room from which she was kidnapped. If she dies, and you did nothing to help me try to find this bastard, I will come back. And at that point it will be to charge you for accessory. But, if you do help me," he thought about his next words carefully, "I'll owe you one."

Nico grinned, "Now we're talking. What do you need to know?"

"I need to know who he is."

"Now, Detective, you of all people should know we don't trade names like that out on the street. But I'll tell you this. He didn't fit my normal clientele. Sure, I sell plenty of skimming devices. But this guy bought the device, some of my best mini cameras, and two fully untraceable phones."

"And how exactly does that help me?"

He smiled again, "While the phones may be untraceable to you guys in law enforcement, I can trace them."

Sampson's mind was racing. This could help him narrow down the location of this sick bastard and bring an end to this.

"While the trace isn't exactly as they make it out to be in the movies, there are some rules that still apply. First and foremost, the phone must be on. If it's powered down, I can't locate it via GPS. But once it's powered on it'll take me five seconds, seven tops to find it."

"How soon can you run this trace?"

"Considering this visit wasn't like I expected, I'd need to access my computer. Once I'm there, the setup to start the trace is instantaneous. The only variable is if your guy has his phone on."

Sampson pulled a card from his pocket, "Call me at this number the minute you have his location narrowed down."

Nico pushed the card away. "No worries, Detective. I'll grab your number. Plus, I wouldn't be caught with your card in my possession. That would be bad for business. When I have a location, I'll reach out to you."

"Thank you," Sampson said as he began walking to the door.

"Don't forget, Detective. You owe me, and best believe I will cash in."

30

T he clock struck 11:00 p.m. when Sampson pulled into the emergency room parking lot. The last update he received from Veronica was that there was nothing new to report. He headed in the direction of the entrance and lamented over the decisions he'd made that lead to this situation.

He should have raised the flag sooner that the killer was still on the loose. Moreover, the killer had been in contact with him on a regular basis. Their technology team could have ran traces on his calls, and maybe they would have caught him by now. But given what he learned from Nico, it was clear that would have been a losing battle.

Still, if more people were out hunting him, Porter wouldn't be in this situation and six of his brothers in blue would not be in the ICU fighting for their lives.

But the reality remained. He hadn't done anything to help them see this maniac was coming for them. And the reason? He wanted to be the one to bring him in. He wanted to prove to himself and everyone else that he was a top-grade detective. He wanted to nab the latest serial killer in the long line of serial killers in this country. It was about him. It was about his ego.

He was headed home when his consciousness told him to stop by the hospital. He needed to see what his inaction had set into motion, and then he would devote the next twenty-one hours to finding Porter and capturing this killer.

Upon entering the hospital, he didn't need to stop and ask where the ICU was located. He knew its location because he'd been there on other occasions. From his fellow officers being shot in the line of duty to rushing that 5-year-old little boy to the hospital in the back of his squad car after being stabbed by one of his friends. He knew his way to the ICU and knew of the misery that spread across the floor. Today, he prayed there would be a little bit of hope to lift the spirts of the family members there asking the Lord for the strength to hold on and to cover their loved ones.

When he arrived on the floor, Captain Marshall was in conversations with the doctor. Sampson began making his way toward the two men when Marshall noticed him. The thought, *what are you doing here,* flashed across his features, but it quickly gave way to solidarity.

"What's the latest?" Sampson asked, joining in on the conversation.

"If you'll excuse me," the doctor said. "I need to attend to my patients." He walked away, leaving the two of them alone.

"Kirby and Torres have already regained consciousness. They are expected to make a full recovery. There's been no change for Martin and Smith, but the doctor is hopeful. Jenkins has been downgraded to critical. They are still trying to determine why he took a turn for the worse. They have additional labs they are preparing to run, and we will know more once that is done. And unfortunately, the doctor is giving Sanchez only a 5% chance to make it through the night."

The last bit stung the most. Sanchez had just been married the previous summer. He and his wife had been trying to conceive, and he was looking forward to having a little daddy's girl.

"The families are in the other room," Marshall continued. "This world can be so unjust at times, and today, this is one of them."

"Any additional leads on the suspect?" Sampson asked.

"None at this time. We found a secret tunnel under the house that led to the house next door. The son of a bitch slipped through our fingers yet again. We're calling in assistance to help with the search. We are burning away too many hours with little to show for our efforts."

"I could always help. Let me help direct the charge, as she's one of our own."

"You can visit with your fallen comrades, but afterward you leave and allow us to handle this."

He wasn't going to get into a spat with Marshall, and he had no intensions of backing down.

In the end he spent an hour visiting with the families and held Mrs. Sanchez in a long embrace. He believed in the power of prayer, so he prayed with her and the other family members in attendance prior to leaving.

He ended up taking the scenic route back to his house so he could clear his head. The pity party he'd thrown for himself had come to an end, and all that was left now was finding Porter. He found his fine motor skills were slow in reacting as he drifted over the line several times. When he arrived at his house, he pondered obtaining a few hours of sleep to recharge or to keep pushing forward. In the end, his body made the decision for him as he fell asleep in his chair pouring over maps of the city.

IT WAS five minutes after 8:00 a.m. when Sampson regained consciousness. The dream he had while asleep was vividly real. In his dream he had an out-of-body experience. One that saw him running at top speed and getting nowhere fast. He'd periodically yell, "Porter! Porter, I'm coming. Where are you?" And each time an answer was never forthcoming. His dream shifted to him running back to the Golden Rock Brewery, the location where Brianna's body was found, a place he'd been before. His spiritual being watched as his physical body entered the building, determined to locate his partner. Inside he noticed a metal door outlined with a white glow. It was clear he was meant to open the door, regardless of what was on the other side. He watched as his body ran to the door, opened it, and stepped inside.

In the middle of the room stood Detective Porter. She was dressed in the same blouse and pants he'd seen her in the day she disappeared. He rushed to her, and she stood unmoving. When he arrived by her side, she glared at him. "You allowed him to get to me," she said, staring into his eyes.

He said, "I know and I'm sorry, we –"

"We were supposed to be looking for him together, and you betrayed me."

He tried to speak again, when he realized this was not a conversation but a monolog.

"If only you'd trusted me. If only you didn't play the game in which he made all the rules. You didn't save Brianna, because you played his game."

Her eyes hardened and with unnatural speed she raised

her hand and poked him three times in the chest before yelling, "Stop playing his game!"

THAT'S WHEN HE AWOKE, face stuck to the map, mouth full of cotton. *I'm going to find you, Elise,* he thought as he oriented himself to his surroundings. The hour and minute hands on the clock were operating with relentless precision. A precision that told him he had less than 12 hours to solve the clues and find Porter.

The vibration of his phone reverberated through the table. He checked the caller ID, *Nico.*

"Tell me you have something," he said in a rush.

"I do. Meet me at Brent's on Trade Street."

TIME WAS DRAWING near on this final act. Would the dashing hero manage to rescue the damsel in distress, or would she become his latest victim? The botched rescue attempt led by the captain added an interesting ring to the story. But it all came down to what Sampson would do. Nonetheless, there was still work he needed to do for the real-life grand finale for his book.

It wasn't lost on him that he still needed a title for his third novel. He'd toyed around with a few, "Abduction," "Rush," "Covert Pursuit," "Last Stand," and a handful more. But none seemed to convey what he was trying to say.

He pushed the thoughts to the back of his mind, because he had a few more preparations to make. He'd go check in on his patient, but the final steps of this choreographed dance needed a few tweaks. For as much grief as he gave the CMPD, for them to follow disparate breadcrumbs to his throwaway persona, they did a decent job. He'd constructed several others in the past three months, but he didn't like to lose any of them. They were a part of him.

After his near capture, he decided to do a little shopping. He needed something more inconspicuous. He picked out a black pair of jeans. A pair of black-on-black running shoes and a black hoodie. He stripped out of his work attire and dawned the new outfit. He folded his work outfit and placed it in the bag the new outfit came out of.

Now that he was dressed in his new attire, it was time to pay the patient a visit. He reflected on the rush he had with his first victim, Mandy, and even his second victim, Brianna. He felt liberated. He felt like he was doing the world some good, because they didn't deserve to walk this Earth any longer.

But the pending demise of Detective Porter was different. He didn't feel any emotion, any release. He thought he'd feel something by the end of the ordeal, and that was yet to be determined, but up to this point there was nothing. It was almost a challenge within himself that he could touch the untouchable. It was something that he wasn't sure Dillon could have pulled off any better than he could.

Let's not get ahead of yourself, the voice said. *You still need to cross the finish line. Don't get complacent and blow this for all of us.* Complacency was the last of his worries. In fact he'd been preparing this final chapter with the highest level of detail.

He ambled over to the bed where Porter was being held, "How are we this morning? Rhetorical question of course. I'm willing to bet you're still waiting on your partner to bust in here in any minute and bring this event to an end. And like I said, I'm rooting for him. In fact, within the next hour, I'm going to give him yet another clue. One that should help to guide him right to you, provided he can solve it. And to show what I good sport I am, I'm going to have it streaming for you so you can check his progress. You may be wondering how that's possible. Don't worry. I've got it covered. But for now, we need to prepare you for the final act."

He positioned the wheelchair next to the bed, and moved her sleeping form into the chair. "Fear not. When the moment comes, you'll be wide awake and won't miss a thing."

31

S ampson paced the inside of Brent's, garnering looks from the other patrons. He rushed right over after he received the call from Nico, and it was now 9:30 and he still had not showed up. Sampson tried calling him several times once he arrived, but the call simply died. No ring on the other end and no voicemail.

He wondered if this was a game that Nico was playing, and if it was he would see to it he brought his entire organization down. He'd see to it that Nico and those he helped to support received hard time for their criminal behavior.

He was just turning to pace toward the back of the space when he caught a glimpse of the door opening. He turned, expecting another let down, when Nico came walking through the door. He bypassed the line for coffee and headed immediately over to Sampson.

"What the hell took you so long?" Sampson asked when he was in earshot.

"There's a booth behind you. Let's chat over there," he said, walking past the detective and going straight for the one in the corner.

Nico slid into the side facing the door, leaving the undesirable side to the detective.

"So, why are you so late?"

"The phone turned on and like I said I immediately put a trace on it. The location didn't make any sense, especially because it wasn't moving. So, I checked to ensure my data was correct, and all signs came back to it being the correct location. I checked it again before coming in, and it's still in the same spot."

"Out with it already, where is he at?"

"He's at Golden Rock Brewery, the place where they found that missing girl, Brianna."

Sampson couldn't believe his ears. *Why on earth would his cell phone be stationary there?* Sampson asked himself.

"I assume you already know how to get there considering you are the one working the case."

"Yes, I know where it's at," he said, standing back up. "Thank you for your assistance."

"My pleasure, Detective. But don't forget, this information isn't free. I've held up my end of the agreement. Make sure when I call for repayment you remember this moment."

Sampson gave a wave that was neither agreement nor dismissal. He needed to get to GRB as quickly as possible knowing that he likely just made a deal with the devil to acquire this information.

He raced to his car and once there thought, *One step closer to finding you. Just hang in there.* He turned on the reds and blues along with the sirens and blew past cars as they pulled aside to let him through. He cleared his mind of the negative thoughts his subconscious tried to plant and focused on the actions he would take.

He would save her...he had to save her.

When he arrived at GRB, there were no cars in sight and

no signs of life. He had a sinking feeling of Déjà vu, but he continued. Without hesitation, he proceeded to the entrance checking his surroundings with each step. He'd learned by now not to underestimate this subject.

He walked in and found the entire floor empty. No chairs, tables, people. Empty. He wondered if he'd already missed him and if so why had he been here. A phone ringing began to echo in the emptiness of the room. In the distance, almost dead center in the space, a glow came from the floor synchronizing with the ring. He raced over and picked it up.

"Yes!"

"I hear the CMPD has recently suffered a shortage of detectives. Everyone knows that can be a dangerous profession."

Sampson began looking around.

"Don't worry, I'm not there. But you are on candid camera. And it's not just me watching you. This feed is being streamed to Detective Porter's location. Now you go ahead and show her that grit and determination, so she doesn't lose hope. Give her a reason to stay strong and hold on, because as I see it you really are her last hope. Since you're on your own, allow me to give you one final clue. Because in the end you'll need to find her one way or another."

Sampson squeezed the phone hard enough he nearly snapped it in two.

He continued, "Sometimes returning to a scene is the only thing you need." And then the connection terminated.

What gibberish is he spewing now? Sampson thought, trying to dissect his words. *Sometimes returning to a scene is the only thing you need.* "The hotel!" he yelled. "Of course, that is where he stashed her. Just like placing Brianna here after I had already searched it."

He then realized how much of a daunting task this would

be. There are 105 rooms on average at a Home2Suite hotel. Coordinating a search on his own would be next to impossible. He retrieved his phone from his pocket and dialed the contact.

"What do you want, Sampson," Marshall asked.

"I think I have a bead on where Porter is being held."

AFTER RECEIVING the intel from Sampson, Captain Marshall decided to play this one by the books. He couldn't afford another misstep in trying to recover his detective if he wanted to continue his bid to be mayor. He'd already called ahead to the Home2Suites general manager for the location Porter was abducted from. He was able to confirm that no one had been booked in room 613. She also guaranteed they'd have access to the room with no interference.

The next part took more negotiations. If Porter wasn't in room 613, they would need to search every room in the hotel. They'd start with the rooms that were vacant and then move to the ones that were occupied. The GM confirmed that of their 112 rooms only twenty-six were vacant. She asked for their discretion in this matter, and he promised they'd be as gentle as they could.

When Marshall and the Mobile Command Unit, MCC, arrived on scene, Sampson was already there, body armor strapped in place. "Just what do you think you're doing?" Marshall asked with contempt in his voice.

"I'm going into that building to see if my partner is in there."

"The hell you are. I've told you I don't want you –"

"I know what you said and the only way you'll stop me is to shoot me, right here, right now."

The S.W.A.T. team had just arrived on scene and were headed to the MCC. Between their starting point and their destination was Sampson and Marshall preparing to square off.

"You follow my lead. No going rogue or playing hero. You got that?"

"When do we start?"

Marshall addressed the men who were approaching, "Who's in charge?"

A bald-headed white man with grey stubble on his chin spoke up, "I am, Sergeant Michael Terry."

The two men shook hands, and Marshall continued, "We need to take this in three stages. First, we check room 613 to see if our detective has been returned to the location she was taken from. This nutjob we are looking for likes to reuse locations that you'd never think to check again. Sampson, I'm going to pair you with Officer Olensky to conduct this search."

"Roger that," Olensky said while Sampson checked his weapon.

"If she isn't in that room, we go to stage two. The general manager has provided us with a list of twenty-six rooms that are unoccupied. Our killer has a device that allows him master key access to the rooms. We need to clear each of those rooms. Sergeant Terry, This is where your team will come into play. I'll leave it to your discretion on how to deploy your men."

"We'll be ready, sir."

"If all else fails, we clear the hotel and check every additional space. This includes conference rooms, the kitchen, and the hotel offices. With any luck our missing detective will be found alive in one of these rooms. Any questions?" he asked as he looked into the eyes of each man.

"Good. Olensky and Sampson, you're up."

The pair walked into the hotel and immediately sought out the GM, who was awaiting their arrival at the counter.

"This is a master key. It'll let you into any room in this hotel. Please remember, discretion. I don't want to panic our patrons unnecessarily."

"Let's pray we don't need to conduct any further searches," Sampson said. "But in case we do, you're going to need a few more of these keys for the remainder of the team."

"I'll have some on standby, good luck."

Sampson headed in the direction of the elevator, followed by Olensky. His mind flashed back to Mandy Cox and Brianna Armstrong. The horrors he inflicted on their bodies. He prayed Porter was not sitting in room 613 having faced a similar fate.

The elevator dinged on the sixth floor, and they made off in the direction of their destination. Sampson gave Olensky the key, "Open the door on my mark," he said and unholstered his weapon.

Olensky prepared the key for entry.

"Now."

He pressed the key against the card reader and pushed the door open. Sampson rushed into the room, weapon drawn, eyes scanning. He filtered quickly, *bed, nightstands, desk, chair, no Porter*. He peeked into the bathroom. *Nothing,*

He called back down to the MCC. "She's not here. Send in S.W.A.T. The GM will have keys for them to search the unoccupied rooms. There are two more on this floor, Olensky and I will take them and the three on five. Have S.W.A.T. start on the top floor working their way down."

He terminated his transmission and said, "Let's go, Olensky."

Rooms 602 and 605 were the other two empty rooms on this floor. The latter would be the closest to their current location and thus the first one they'd check. They replicated the entry as before, Olensky unlocking and opening the door, Sampson going in first. And just like before, nothing. They closed the door behind them and proceeded to the final room on this floor. Same result.

Over the comms, the other members of this search party called off the rooms they cleared. As Sampson and Olensky ran down the stairs to the fifth floor, Sampson replayed the words from the suspect, *sometimes returning to a scene is the only thing you need.* Something about the statement was tugging at him, but he couldn't place his finger on it.

When they arrived on the fifth floor, an elderly couple stepped aside as these two serious looking men rushed down the hall. At the first room on this floor 507, they repeated the cycle and again nothing. The "all clears" continued to ring over the comms as they pushed onto the next room.

Olensky and Sampson finished up the fifth floor without any sign of Porter. "Captain, she's not in any of the vacant rooms on floors five or six." Everyone else chimed in and confirmed that the vacant rooms were all clear. Marshall came on the comms, "Hold one while we prepare for stage three."

Stage three would mean a building evacuation and officers at every exit. It was the job of those officers to check each person exiting the building looking for someone who fit the physical description of their suspect. They were also advised to keep an eye out for a man with a laceration on his face.

Sampson looked down at his watch. *This is taking too much time.* It was his hunch that brought everyone to this building and now an exhaustive search was being conducted. Yet the uneasy feeling in his gut insisted something wasn't right.

"We're in position," Marshall stated. The GM will call for a building evacuation. Be on the lookout for anything or anyone suspicious. Once the evacuation is complete, go through the remaining rooms."

Two minutes later, the PA system came to life, "Guests, please prepare to exit the building in an orderly fashion. Once you are on ground level, we will advise you of where to go. I repeat, please prepare to exit the building. We ask that you do this in an orderly and safe fashion."

Sampson prepared for the panic that would ensue regardless of the request for order. Human nature would want to know what is going on, and in the face of little information the mind filled in the worst-possible solution.

He and Olensky were still on the fifth floor when patrons began exiting their rooms. Most headed for the stairwell, figuring that would be the best route out, while others fought against the masses to head for the elevator. Sampson spotted the elderly couple being jostled while they tried for the elevator.

Sampson joined the crowd headed toward the stairwell and connected with the couple. "I'll help you," he said gently taking the woman's hand. He turned around and said, "CMPD, make way." Marshall still had his badge, so the only thing providing proof of his claim was the vest he wore.

It took a second command before the group pressed up against the right-hand side of the hall, clearing a passage for Sampson and the couple. "I'm going to help them downstairs," he said to Olensky. "I'll be right back up, and we can start our search." Olensky gave him a nod and continued to monitor the traffic.

The elevator car doors were just about to close by the time they reached it. Sampson thrust his hand through the opening, forcing the doors back open. There was a young girl, early twenties, on crutches leaning against the back of the car.

Sampson escorted the couple in and pressed the door close button.

The young woman looked over at Sampson and asked, "What's this all about?" He wasn't aware of the cover story that was going to be used so he just said, "You'll find out more once we are on ground level." The expression on her face said she wasn't convinced, but she also didn't ask any additional questions.

On the ground floor, Sampson exited with the elderly couple and the young lady crutched out behind them. The woman spoke, "Thank you so much, young man. We surely do appreciate your assistance."

"You're welcome," Sampson said as he turned to hop back on the elevator. He heard the old man say, "Since we're down here, we might as well go check on our renovations." The statement stopped him in his tracks.

Sometimes returning to a scene is the only thing you need, played through his mind one more time. *This isn't the scene he was referring to.* He turned around and sprinted toward the exit. The mass of humanity prevented him from running a straight line to his car, yet somehow Marshall must have noticed him. "Sampson, what in the hell are you doing down here? You are supposed to be inside conducting the search."

"She's not here. The scene that she's been returned to is her new home."

32

Troy Evans watched as the Home2Suites was being evacuated. He'd followed Sampson to this location from GRB. It hadn't been a hard follow. Sampson carried with him the phone that was left at the old brewery. Furthermore, he trailed him on the motorcycle he'd purchased a while back. Dressed in his jeans, sweatshirt and helmet, it was highly unlikely he'd garner enough attention for him to worry. And with Sampson's mind preoccupied, checking his surroundings was the last of his worries.

He had to admit he was disappointed but not surprised. He felt the clue was sufficient to lead him to Porter. But when you don't look for the deeper meanings and only stay surface level, you're bound to miss so much. And yet again, Sampson was only thinking on the surface.

As more and more guests filed out from the hotel the time on this adventure was drawing to a close. That's when he noticed a man in a CMPD vest running through the parking lot. It only took a second glance to realize it was Sampson. It appeared he was headed to his car, so Troy fired up his motorcycle and continued to watch.

When Sampson dropped behind the wheel, he started the engine, turned on the lights and sirens and sped off. Recognizing the car was pointed in the right direction, Troy said, "It's about time."

SAMPSON HAD PULLED up Porter's new address from his GPS's recently taken trips when he left the hotel. Again, he'd been kicking himself for not seeing this earlier. It didn't matter. It was clear now, and he was headed to rescue his partner.

With each rev of the engine, his adrenaline spiked. The GPS said he was three minutes away, but with the speed he was carrying it was likely closer to one.

"Hold on partner. I'm almost there." He slowed enough to make the next turn and accelerated out of it. Ahead of him on the right he could see Porter's home. He blew through the stop sign and then slammed on the breaks, skidding to a stop outside of her home. He thew the door open and in one fluid motion began running around the hood of his car while simultaneously drawing his weapon. As he ran, he tried to remember the code Porter set for the door. He searched his memory, but he couldn't recall it. He picked up his speed, abandoning the six-digit code she'd set and instead opting for brute force.

There was a minute lip of a step leading from the walking path to the porch. He had to be cautious to time his steps not to trip on it, but nothing that would break his stride. As his foot made contact with the porch, he lowered his shoulder and plowed through the door.

It gave way instantly from the power he generated on his approach and the extra force he gave it upon contact. The door jamb shattered on impact along with one of the hinges as the door swung inwardly. He managed to regain control quickly enough to see a sight that stopped him dead in his tracks.

In the center of the room positioned for him to see sat Detective Elise Porter. She had an IV attached to her right arm, and her head was slouched to the side.

He stowed his weapon. "Oh my God, Elise," he said, rushing over to her. "What has this bastard done to you?" Her skin, while still attached to her body, was clammy and pale white. It was hot to the touch, and she had perspiration building on her brow. He searched for a pulse, nothing. He pressed harder, and it was there but faint.

He pulled the phone from his pocket and dialed. On the first ring it was answered, "Dispatch, this is Veronica."

"Veronica, it's Sampson. I've found Porter, she's at 2821 Turtle Drive and is in bad shape. Send EMS crews immediately." He hung up the phone realizing he hadn't cleared the home. He pulled his gun back out and jumped to his feet.

The place was still empty as she hadn't moved in yet, but he knew he should check the closets and other rooms of the house. He made quick work of the first floor and ran upstairs. Each of the rooms on the second floor were clear as well. He ran back downstairs remembering that unlike most homes in North Carolina, Porter's had a basement. He hurried over to the door and pulled it open.

When he reached the bottom, his breath was caught in his throat. A table, drawer, and bed were situated down there. The bed had restraints where she was likely being held until the moment she was posed at the door. He cleared the basement, again with frustrations setting in. *Why didn't I ever think of looking here?*

He raced back to the main floor and tried to revive her. "Porter. I'm here. Can you hear me?" She didn't respond. He realized the IV was still pushing liquid into her system. The bag was unmarked, so he didn't know if it was keeping her alive or killing her slowly. He decided it didn't matter—this psychopath couldn't be trusted. He slid the needle from her arm and pushed away the cart.

In his ear, over the comms that he forgot was there, was the voice of Marshall. If he could hear his voice, that meant Veronica had spread the news and they were all descending on this location.

"Sampson, can you hear me?"

"Yes, I hear you."

"We're on our way there, only a few minutes out. How is she?"

"Barely breathing. Where is that damn ambulance?"

"They're on the way. Any sign of the perp?"

"No, no sign of him. The place is cleared. Looks like he was holding her in the basement."

The wailing sirens sounded like they were a block or two away. Sampson ran to the shattered door and spotted the flashing lights headed his direction. He willed them to move faster as he looked back at the still-slumped form of his partner. His wish was answered as they pulled into the driveway, and the EMT hoped out the back.

"I'm Detective Sampson with the CMPD. Inside is my partner, Detective Porter. She's unconscious and her pulse is thready." As he began to usher them into the house, the Mobile Command Unit pulled up. He let the EMTs go to Porter while he awaited the appearance of Marshall.

"EMT's just arrived," he said as Marshall walked into the house. They both stood back watching as they attempted to revive her. One finally spoke and said, "We need to get her to the hospital stat. They expertly transported her body to the rolling bed, lifted it to its full height, and headed for the door.

Marshall and Sampson followed in their wake. Additional patrol cars were appearing on the scene while they loaded Porter into the van.

"I'm going with her," he said to the technician.

"Sir, we can't…"

"I'm going with her," he said, menace in his voice and fire in his eyes.

The technician stepped backward, giving him space to hop in the back. The driver, who Sampson hadn't noticed before, closed the door and jogged back to the front. He dropped the vehicle in gear, started up the sirens, and sped off.

The techs had cut Porter's shirt open and were attaching leads so they could read her heartbeat. *Come on, you've got to make it*, Sampson said to himself. He watched as the pulse was slowing and slowing.

"Give her a shot of adrenaline," the one tech said to the other. He reached into the drawer, extracted the shot, placed it against her skin and pressed. "It had no effect. BP's dropping too."

Sampson was frozen in space and could only look as they tried to save her life.

"We're losing her," the tech said as her heartbeat slowed further. "Charge the paddles."

The van made a sharp turn that caused Sampson to lose his balance, but it didn't phase the two working on his partner. Over the sound of the sirens wailing and the techs yelling, he heard the unmistakable sound of the machine reporting Porter's heart had flatlined.

They shocked her once, twice, and once on full power and there wasn't a bleep. One of them checked both of her pupils, and neither was reactive to light. The tech holding the paddles said, "I'm sorry, sir. He looked down at his watch. Pronouncing time of death at 8:01 p.m."

"No!" came the guttural sound deep from within Sampson's core as he collapsed on top of his partner.

EPILOGUE

Three days after Porter's death, a funeral was held in her honor. Her old unit from Asheville came down to Charlotte to participate. Her mom, sister, and brother were all in attendance. The service had been tastefully done, and in the end there wasn't one dry eye in the place.

At the burial site, Sampson led the other five pallbearers as they carried the casket and sat it next to the hole that had been dug as her final resting place. Sampson tried his best to hold it together, but in his mind he could only blame himself for what happened to her. And Marshall didn't make it any easier. He was now on indefinite suspensions pending further investigations into his conduct.

In his mind, he didn't care. He couldn't see working any other case until the person responsible for her death was laying in the ground as well. Then and only then would he rest. Since finding her, the killer had been eerily silent.

At the conclusion of the ceremonies at the burial site, Sampson took off without speaking to anyone else. He'd driven around for over an hour without a destination in mind. That was until he ended up at the gates leading into the Driftwood Springs community. The gate operator recognized who he was and opened it without any additional questions.

He weaved his way back to 300 Calgary Lane, parked his car, and stepped out. It had been a while since he stopped by, and he hoped his visit would be welcome. He rang the door-bell and began pacing back and forth. It took only a few moments before Special Agent Donatella Dabria answered the door.

He rushed into the house, skipping all pleasantries. Nervous energy radiated from his body as he continued to pace once he was inside. When she closed the door, he stopped, turned to her, and said, "Donatella, you've heard about the coed who had been killed and skin removed from her body."

She shook her head and said, "Yes, and if I recall you captured the killer."

"Well, that's just it. The person we have behind bars could not have perpetrated this crime."

She looked at him, trying to anticipate where he was going, but his mind seemed to be all over the place.

"A few weeks back, another coed was killed with the same MO."

"A copycat?" she asked to which he shook his head.

"No, that was the original line of thinking by the powers that be, but I knew better and tried to tell them. After we made the initial arrest, I received a call from a guy saying he was the killer, and the man we had behind bars for the murder deserved to be in jail because of various other activities he participated in. Anyway, I truly wish I could say that was the last time he struck, but that would be a lie."

He took a deep breath and locked eyes with the agent. "Donatella, he has struck again, elevating his status to that of a serial killer. This last crime scene was the worst one of all. I'm coming to you because I need your help. There is a high degree of certainty the FBI will be called in, and if that is the case I want to work with someone I trust and someone I know can get the job done. I want to work with you."

He felt her appraising him and the statements he was making. She knew all too well that need to rectify a wrong at all costs, and it was with that knowledge he hoped he could spur her into action. She had a similar look when she was hunting another serial killer, Terri Buckley, and when she decided to find those responsible for killing her parents. While she didn't do partners, he hoped in this one instance she would make an exception. She looked at him and asked, "Where do we start?"

The End

IF YOU ENJOYED "COVERT PURSUIT," please consider leaving a **review** so that other readers just like you can locate this novel.

NOTES FROM THE AUTHOR

Thank you for your purchase of Covert Pursuit, the second novel in the Detective Sampson Series. I'm always humbled when someone takes the time to read my work and appreciate your continued support.

In constructing this story, the question I kept trying to answer, how do you turn the predator into the prey. It had a certain duality to it that I like. Certainly, everyone sees Troy as the predator, but because of his crimes, he's being hunted, and rightfully so, by the police. In his mind, going after the people coming after him was the ultimate satisfaction.

Midway through the book, we begin to witness Troy losing touch with reality and listening to the voices in his head. So much so that there was a part in which his subconscious took over and Troy was relegated to a corner in his own mind. It's here were he also starts to recognize that he's losing control.

I anticipate much will be made about the fate of Detective Elise Porter, and to be fair, I went back and forth on what the reunion would be like. One morning, the scene that took place in the ambulance came to me and it was then her fate was sealed. At the time I was midway through writing the book, but it helped to fuel the remaining direction.

The question now, what will happen with Detective Sampson? That is a loaded question. He's been bested by this killer multiple times, his partner has been murdered and now he's sought the assistance of Special Agent Donatella Dabria. This partnership has been one in the making since the second book in the Donatella Series, **Hour of Reckoning**. This is where we are first introduced to both Detective Sampson and Troy Evans.

Why is this important? Every novel across both series has led to a Donatella and Detective Sampson crossover event unlike anything you have seen. More details will be forthcoming and if you want to be in the know, be sure you are subscribed to my **newsletter.** Thank you once again for your continued support.

Sincerely
Demetrius Jackson